THE KING STONE

THE EARTH GRID SERIES BOOK 1

S.A. BECK

PROLOGUE

THE STONE CIRCLE shone softly under the light of a full moon. The English sky was clear, the moon and stars shining cold and distant. A bone-white glow covered the land.

Twenty robed figures stood around the stones, their arms raised. Together they intoned a chant not heard in hundreds of years, one unknown even to most advanced students of the occult arts.

One that most who delved into the hidden world wouldn't dare utter.

At the dead center of the stone circle, a man lay bound and gagged. His brown skin was slick with sweat, and his eyes bugged out as he glanced in panic at the men and women chanting around him. He looked for pity. He looked for hope. He looked for any sign that this was a cruel joke and he would soon be set free.

He looked in vain.

The chanting stopped. A trim, handsome man in his fifties with graying sideburns called out to his fellow cultists.

"Tonight we strike the first blow that will lead to our liberation. Tonight we start the war. For a time, it will be a silent war, fought in secret. Our enemies will not even know we are fighting them. They will continue to think their invasion of our land is all but complete. They will laugh about how they are replacing us. But they do not know of this land's power. A power invested in its ancient sites and tied together through the power of the ley lines."

"We must arise! We must fight! We are the vanguard of a new English army!" the cultists chanted.

"It is time for us to make a sacrifice," said the man with the graying temples. "Time for us to give something to the ley lines so they will give back to us. Who will conduct the sacrifice?"

There was a long silence. The cult leader frowned.

He was about to speak when a woman about his age who stood to his right spoke up.

"I will."

The man looked at her and nodded. "You are brave and a true warrior."

She smiled and flushed, basking in his approval.

The woman pulled a curved knife from beneath her robes and held it aloft. The keen blade gleamed in the moonlight.

The leader raised his hands. "We must all chant the spell as she makes the sacrifice. It will open the ley line to receive the foreign blood she shall spill for this land."

The chanting resumed. The woman walked into the center of the circle, trembling a little.

She stood over the bound and gagged figure. He looked up at her, shaking his head violently.

"You should have stayed in Pakistan," she told him. Her voice wavered, only a little.

The next instant she brought the knife down. Her weak, hasty thrust glanced off the man's ribs. He screamed through his gag, the cry of pain drowned out by the rising chant.

She stabbed again, this time driving the blade deep into his gut. She wrenched the blade to one side, her eyes clenched tight, then drove it up behind the sternum and into the heart.

With a sob, she yanked the knife free. Blood

spilled onto the grass and the hem of her robe. The woman stood, composed herself, and walked unsteadily back to the man who had called for a volunteer.

The chant ended.

The leader smiled at her. She smiled back, trembling a little.

"You have done well, my love." He turned to address the others. "The spell has begun. At the next full moon, it will be time for the next step. Then the reconquest of our land will begin. We will all be warriors in the great war to take England back."

The robed men and women cheered.

"We'll be seeing plenty more of their kind end up like this," one of them joked, pointing to the dead immigrant at the center of the stone circle.

The leader nodded and smiled. "You will, I promise you. There will be blood enough, and for once it will be all theirs instead of ours."

"I think I have found a new one to join our ranks," a middle-aged woman standing beside the leader said.

"It's too sensitive a time to initiate anyone," the leader replied.

"She's got the Talent," the woman said. "And

she's right under my thumb. Let me work on her. She could be a great asset."

The leader considered for a moment then nodded.

"All right. We will have to approach her with care. I know a way. Work on her, and then introduce me to her. We may be able to bend her to our will and use her in the fight to come."

"And if not?" another woman asked.

"Then we will force her," the leader replied. "Or kill her."

1

DELLA MARSHAL WIPED the sweat from her brow and returned to clearing soil from the Bronze Age grave with her trowel. She had to take care. The funerary urn containing the ashes of some man or woman now dead for almost four thousand years was already half exposed, the ashes within hidden by an upturned ceramic bowl that acted as a lid. She hadn't touched the urn. Investigating the contents had to wait for the lab. In the meantime, the earth around the urn needed to be scraped away centimeter by centimeter while she kept a lookout for stray finds. Generally, the Bronze Age people only put artifacts inside the urns—like some amber beads or a copper bracelet—but with so many centuries of rodents burrowing through the soil, the cycles of freeze and thaw, and scattered trash from the time, one always had to be careful. Artifacts could be found at any spot in the soil.

Her caution paid off. As she scraped, the edge of her trowel uncovered a potsherd. She held it up and smiled. To most people, it looked like a small bit of old ceramic half the size of the palm of her hand. To a graduate student at the School of Archaeology at the University of Oxford, it was a rim sherd, a portion of the lip of the vessel. These, along with portions of the shoulder and base, were called "diagnostic sherds," parts that hinted at the shape of the whole. Since the entire sequence of pottery styles in the Bronze Age had been detailed down to the century or even half century, this little bit of pottery could be assigned a date.

Della knew, without having to look it up in one of the ponderous volumes in the Bodleian Library, that this was from a small bowl dating to the earlier part of the Bronze Age, about 1550 BC.

She put it back where she had found it, then picked up the grid paper map she used to draw the one-meter-by-one-meter square she was working in, and pinpointed the exact location and depth.

Once she had it recorded on the map, she put the

sherd in a plastic Ziploc bag and marked the information on the plastic with a Sharpie.

Della stood. That was a lucky find, one that would make her professor, Dr. Patricia Olding, "quite happy." The English were always "quite" happy or "quite" upset, or "perhaps a bit excited." Typical English understatement. As a "Yank" she was considered "quite the opposite," even though she was a bookish archaeology nerd. These people should see some of the girls she had gone to school with. Then they'd understand what outspoken was.

The date for the potsherd was the latest yet found on the site, lengthening the known use of this burial ground by a century.

And what a site! She looked out over the open field, which felt warm and pleasant in the summer sun. Right around her was a crew of a dozen graduate students and local pensioners who volunteered for the summer's work, each busy at some task in the small patch of Bronze Age cemetery they excavated.

Just fifty meters beyond stood a stone circle called the King's Men, made up of seventy-seven stones set closely together to make a circle some thirty-three meters in diameter. It dated to 2,500 BC, the transition time from the Late Neolithic to the Early Bronze

Age. Beyond stood a cluster of taller stones called the Whispering Knights, the remains of an old burial chamber for some long-forgotten chieftain who had died almost a thousand years before the stone circle was erected. Through a screen of trees and past a two-lane country road stood the King Stone, a tall, jagged stone erected around the same time someone had broken that pot she discovered. It was the youngest megalith on the site but looked the oldest, being much pitted by the elements and covered with lichen. The entire site was collectively called the Rollright Stones.

Della smiled. This was like a dream come true for her. Back when she was a little girl in New York, she'd pester her parents to take her to the Metropolitan Museum of Art to see medieval swords and ancient Egyptian mummies. She devoured books on cave art and stone circles. She had once corrected her sixth-grade history teacher when he said Stone-henge was a unique monument. It was not, she proudly told him. There were some thousand stone circles in the British Isles, and Stonehenge wasn't even the largest or oldest.

That had gotten her sent to the principal's office for talking back. Her parents had intervened, brought books that showed she was right, and got an apology from the teacher. Her parents were cool that way.

The incident had taught her an important lesson —just because someone was in a position of authority, didn't mean they knew what they were talking about.

"You done with that?"

A male voice snapped her out of her reverie. It was Angus, a Scottish pensioner and one of the volunteers with the dig. Red-faced and sporting a big beer belly, he knew as much about drinking as he did about archaeology, but he was a sweetie. He was like a big, graying, hard-drinking teddy bear.

He pointed to the plastic bucket of earth she had so meticulously scraped out of her square. On the side of the bucket was written her square number.

"Yeah, go ahead and take it," Della said.

"You coming to the Bookbinder's Arms when we're done?" he asked.

It was one of the crew's favorite pubs.

"Um, sure," she said, tensing. She cursed herself for saying yes. Her reaction was automatic, being agreeable to an agreeable person, and the exact opposite of what she wanted to say. She wondered if she could get out of it.

He gave her a thumbs-up, picked up the bucket,

and walked over to a metal screen with wooden sides standing on two moveable legs. Called a sift, it was used to filter the soil in search of smaller artifacts the person excavating the square might have missed. Angus poured the bucket of soil in the screen and started shaking it back and forth. The soil filtered through the screen, helped along by Angus's beefy hand pushing the moist clods through.

Della got back to work. It was already late in the day, and she wanted to get this funerary urn out of the ground. It wasn't a good idea to leave artifacts exposed during the night. Rain could seep through the tarp they put over the excavation every evening, and even worse, some idiot might come along and steal it. Vandalism was a big problem at ancient sites. A few years ago, Dr. Olding had told her, someone had daubed yellow paint all over the King Stone and several other stones.

Of course, at this point, she could simply pull the urn out of the ground. It was already more than half exposed. But that would be treasure hunting, not archaeology. Context—the layer of soil, the artifact's location in relation to other artifacts, its position in the ground—meant everything. All of that information added up to make a clearer picture of the past.

Angus stomped over in his Wellington boots,

returning the empty bucket and handing her a little piece of flint.

"Another piece of the puzzle," he said, and went off to sift someone else's dirt.

She bagged the flint. It was just a waste flake, a bit that some ancient craftsman broke off a flint nodule while making a dagger or arrowhead. But, as Angus said, it was a piece of the puzzle.

And Della loved puzzles.

The rest of the afternoon flew by, the quiet sounds of scraping trowels and the *shush shush* of the sift punctuated by low conversation and one cheer as Nigel, a fellow graduate student, came across a bronze arrowhead.

But for the most part Della worked alone and in peace, the rich smell of the earth filling her nostrils, her eyes alert for any discovery. She scraped down the rest of her square until the cinerary urn stood totally exposed. The soil had produced little, a few waste flakes and a couple of body sherds, portions of old vessels that were not diagnostic and thus would be difficult to date.

As the light began to fade, Dr. Olding came over and took a photograph of the cinerary urn, and together they gently lifted the urn into a large bag for later examination in the lab. The lid, closed for millennia, would be opened, and the remains of the bones examined. With any luck, they might find a bronze bracelet or some amber beads traded all the way from the Baltic.

At last the day's work was complete. Della felt the usual sense of disappointment that a job she loved was over and the satisfaction that she had done it well. Tomorrow she'd get back to work, making more discoveries and learning more about the past.

Dr. Olding helped her put the tarp over her section of the excavation.

"Nigel and Hannah are down on the next soil strata," her professor told her as they weighed down the edge of the tarp with stones. "Not much there. It looks like the time period of this cemetery wasn't too long. We'll have you go down another twenty centimeters, and if you don't find much of interest, we'll have you open up another square."

"All right. Are you coming to the Bookbinder's Arms?" Della asked.

"No. I have something to do."

Della felt a tug of disappointment. Dr. Olding was all work, which was why Della wanted her to come to the pub. She wanted to talk shop. Instead the others would talk about football or music stars or all the other things she didn't understand.

Taking a deep breath, Della headed to the porta-potty at the edge of the excavation. She entered the foul-smelling booth, closed and locked the plastic door behind her, and put her face in her hands.

"It's not that big of a deal," she whispered to herself. "Just a couple of pints with kind, interesting people. None of them will judge you. None of them will dislike you."

She knew the words were true, and she knew she could never get herself to believe them.

All she wanted to do was stay in here until she heard the cars start up one by one and drive away. She wanted to wait until the sun set and come out to find herself alone amidst the stones. Then she could drive back to her little flat, eat alone, and spend the night watching TV or reading a book.

But no, she had to say yes to having pints with a bunch of people who wished her nothing but well.

Della clenched her hands into fists tight enough that her nails, though they were trimmed close to avoid picking up too much dirt, jabbed into the palms of her hands.

A few deep breaths of foul air calmed her, and she managed a little laugh. Hiding in this funky little toilet was a good motivator. The way some of the guys left the porta-potty, she'd brave a dozen rounds at the loudest pub rather than stay in here.

She squared her shoulders. At least she'd have the drive back to Oxford to herself.

The Bookbinder's Arms was a friendly pub on the west side of Oxford. A popular place, it was crowded with an early-evening crowd who took up all the barstools and most of the tables. The excavation crew was lucky enough to get the long table in the back room to themselves. Graduate students and volunteers crowded around, some having to pinch chairs from other parts of the pub to get everyone in. Della found herself crushed between Angus and Evelyn, a French graduate student. Evelyn was twenty-three, the same age as Della, and what American men would call "hot" and British men would call "fit." Della used to resent good-looking women for always seeming more confident than she was. Now she felt grateful because they deflected much of the attention.

Della sipped her pint of strong British beer and let the conversation wash around her. Nigel chatted up Evelyn, as did every other male in earshot except Angus, who had enough self-respect to understand that his age meant he wasn't in the running. Instead, he relayed some local folklore to Della and two other graduate students—Hannah, a boisterous Ph.D. student with straw-colored hair and a nose already red at age twenty-seven from too much drinking; and Winston, a first-year master's student at age twenty-two, who with his thick glasses, stammer, and awkward social mannerisms made him look like Della felt.

"Now, the interesting thing about this place we're digging," Angus said, "is the story attached to it. You see, a king and his men were marching through the countryside long, long ago when who did they meet but Old Mother Shipton, the most famous of English witches."

"I thought that was Dr. Olding!" Hannah cackled. She was already on her third pint, and Della suspected she had downed a shot while she was at the bar.

"Steady," Angus said. "Now, this wasn't a king of England we're talking about. This was in the early days when the land was a patchwork of little kingdoms, with every petty ruler dreaming of uniting all the land under their own rule. Old Mother Shipton faced the king and issued him a challenge. According to the folklore, she intoned:

'Seven long strides thou shalt take, says she
And if Long Compton thou canst see,

King of England thou shalt be!'"

"What's Long Compton?" Hannah asked.

"It's a village down in the valley near the site," Angus said. "Well, the king's army got in a circle to discuss this, and after a bit, they decided the king should try his luck. The king took seven long steps forward, but a bit of rising ground still blocked his view of the valley.

"Old Mother Shipton let out a gleeful laugh and said,

'As Long Compton thou canst not see,

King of England thou shalt not be!

Rise up stick and stand still stone,

For King of England thou shalt be none;

Thou and thy men hoar stones shall be,

And I myself an elder tree!'"

"So, they all turned to stone," Hannah said. "I guess the Whispering Knights are some more of his men?"

"Indeed they are," Angus replied. "The reason they stand apart is because they were trailing a bit behind the march, conspiring against their sovereign."

The reason they stand apart is because they were part of a Neolithic dolmen and the rest of the site was made in the early Bronze Age, Della said to herself.

"Th-that's a good story," Winston said. "M-maybe it's an old f-folk memory of the d-dolmen. It w-would have been a t-t-tomb for a local k-king."

"I don't think the locals are going to remember something from that long ago," Hannah snapped.

Winston cringed a little and didn't reply. Della felt sorry for him. She did that too when people criticized her.

"I wouldn't be so sure," Angus said, taking another long pull from his glass. "Folk memory can last for a very long time. A recent anthropological report from Australia found that a tribe of Aborigines living near the coast said that a sacred rock just offshore used to be connected with the mainland. Divers went down and discovered that there's a spit of land just under the surface of the water connecting the rock with the mainland. The last time it was connected with the mainland was when the sea levels were lower forty thousand years ago."

"Wow," Della blurted. "That's incredible."

She blushed as everyone looked at her. She preferred to be silent in crowds so everyone forgot she was there. Actually, she preferred not to be in crowds at all.

Angus raised his glass, as if toasting her decision to finally join the conversation.

"England is an old land," he said. "Just like Aboriginal Australia. People tell stories down the generations, and while the details change, and the stories get prettied up with magic and adventure, a kernel of truth always remains. Like what Winston said, the local folk have remembered that the site was a royal burial." Winston gave the Scotsman a grateful grin.

"But I haven't finished with my story. When the moon is full, or if there's a saint's day, it is said that the King Stone comes alive, and that the king walks around the site of the Rollright Stones, trying to awaken his old army. And did you know that tonight there's a full moon? Not only that, but it's June 11th, the Feast of St. Barnabas, an important day in the old medieval calendar."

"Oooh, spoooooky!" Hannah said, wiggling her fingers in the air.

Angus cocked his head and looked at her. "It's also said that the king likes to lop the heads off of unbelieving uni students. Now, if you don't mind, I think I'll get another pint."

"Me too," Hannah said, the idea of another drink overriding any embarrassment she might have felt at the dressing-down she'd just received.

When they left, Winston turned to Della.

"W-what do you think?"

"I think he might have a point, but in the end, we still need to do a scientific investigation if we want to learn anything concrete about the past."

Winston nodded. "A f-fun s-story, though."

Della had almost finished her pint and did not want another round. She'd fulfilled her social obligation, and now she could get out of there. She decided to call Sebastian, her boyfriend.

How she had gotten such a kind and easygoing guy to fall for her was beyond her understanding. Sebastian was a graduate student in the classics department and the same age as she was. He was bookish like her but also good at football and very handsome with his shock of black hair and soft brown eyes. They read books together, went to the theater down in London, and spent lots of quiet evenings in her little flat.

One thing she really appreciated was that he wasn't demanding physically. In fact, they hadn't had sex at all. They just traded long back rubs and snuggled together under the sheets all night. If she slept late, Sebastian would wake her with breakfast in bed. She wouldn't mind a bit more on the physical side, but Sebastian seemed strangely hesitant, and Della had decided not to spoil a good thing.

She reached into her purse to get her phone and let out a curse.

"W-what's the m-matter?"

"I left my phone on the site. I took a couple of photos of the urn and didn't put it back. What an idiot I am!"

"Y-you b-better get it. It's s-s-supposed to rain tonight."

"Right."

She said her goodbyes and hurried out.

It was dark when she left the pub. She got into her car, a compact little two-door Nissan, and headed out of town. The drive was short and the rain hadn't started, so she told herself her phone would be fine.

But what a dumb move. The words of her high school math teacher came back to her.

"Why do you want to be an archaeologist, Della? You should be an astronaut. You're a total space cadet."

Nice. A really appropriate thing for a high school teacher to say to a withdrawn teenage girl with self-confidence problems.

Sad thing was, the guy was right. She really was a space cadet. She couldn't count the number of times she'd locked herself out of her flat or her car.

She'd even given Sebastian spare keys just in case. He had to save her more than once.

"Aargh!" she shouted. She had just missed the turnoff. Space case for sure.

It didn't matter. She could park by the road and cut across the field. It was all open grassland except for the preserved area around the site, and there was no fence.

She parked, grumbling to herself, and started walking across the field, her work boots pressing into the soft earth. She'd have to pass the King Stone, cross the little country lane she had missed, and enter the excavation area. The moon rose in the east, big and full and casting a silvery sheen over the fields. Only a few clouds scudded across the sky. If rain came tonight, it wouldn't be for a while yet. She relaxed as she breathed in the warm summer air and listened to the peaceful silence of the night.

A light up ahead made her pause. The light shone in the direction of the site, which lay hidden behind some trees. Then it appeared behind the trees too, winking in and out of sight. Someone was walking around the excavation.

Pothunters? Della's heart began to beat faster. Thieves sometimes came to archaeological sites to steal. Some ancient artifacts were worth big money on the black market.

And here she was without a phone to call the cops.

Summoning her courage, she crept forward. At least she might be able to get a peek at what they were doing and give the police a description. Or maybe it was just some kids partying. She hoped so.

The ground was soft and muffled her footsteps. The sound of voices came to her, and she thought she detected several dark shapes beyond the trees. The light stopped moving and then winked out.

She paused. What was going on over there? Pothunters would keep the light on to work. Maybe it was just a bunch of kids making out and smoking weed?

Della had half convinced herself that she should leave when the chanting started.

It came low and sinister, rolling across the empty field to clench Della's heart.

Everything told her to run, but she had to see. That curiosity, that need to know the truth behind any mystery that had dominated her entire life, pulled her forward.

She passed through the trees, taking care with

every step so that she didn't snap a twig underfoot and give herself away.

The scene came into view. The King Stone stood in the moonlight, looking like a hunched old man in a gray cloak. Around it stood thirteen figures in white robes, their heads bare, their arms upraised. They did not wear hoods, and in the moonlight, Della could see their features clearly.

"Oh, power of the Earth, obey my commands!" intoned one figure, a lean man with graying sideburns who looked to be in his fifties. "We are here on this sacred day to tap into the power of your majesty."

"Oh, power of the Earth, obey our commands," the others repeated.

Della's breath caught. She recognized one of the people in robes.

It was Dr. Patricia Olding, the head of the excavation and her graduate supervisor.

Panic nearly overwhelmed her curiosity. It took all her willpower to keep from making a noisy retreat through the trees.

Della crept away and made a big detour to get to the excavation site. Luckily, it was separated from the King Stone by more trees, and she vanished from sight as she reached her square. The chanting continued all the while. She felt under the tarp and found her phone where she had left it, just at the square's edge.

She grabbed the phone and sprinted for her car.

As she did, the chanting increased in pitch behind her, and the entire area around the King Stone was suffused in a golden glow that cast slim beams like fingers through the trees.

2

LUCAS LANCASTER SANDED the leg of the chair he worked on, an imitation of the clean lines and perfect finish of the Georgian era. The chair stood atop a work table in his shed on his aunt and uncle's farm. Lucas breathed in the rich smells of wood shavings and paint, his mind at ease.

If only it could always be like this.

At twenty-four, Lucas had nothing in his life but two kindly relations and a talent for woodwork. He told himself it was enough.

And, for brief periods of solitude in his work-shop, it was enough.

He studied the chair, his expert eye searching for any flaw, any irregularity. No, it was coming along perfectly. It was one of a set for a lord in Pembrokeshire, replacements for the originals that had finally decayed with time. Aristocracy, museums, the occasional nouveau riche customer with taste, all bought Lucas's craftsmanship for exorbitant prices. Among a small circle of aficionados, he was famous.

Although, of course, he was never one of them. Britain's class lines took care of that. Even the museum curators, who made less than he did, were Oxford- or Cambridge-educated and living more off inheritances than anything they earned with their own labor.

Lucas shoved those thoughts aside. They disturbed his fragile peace.

For another hour he worked, sanding, touching up, until the chair stood perfect, the exact likeness of those great works of craft made three hundred years ago.

Time for tea.

He knew this instinctively. The workshop had no clock, and he owned no watch. He didn't want the damn things around, and they always broke in his presence. Apparently, they didn't want him around either. Because of this mutual antipathy, he had developed a keen sense of time and could tell the time within a quarter of an hour, even when he was in the creative zone for the past two hours and eleven minutes.

Give or take five minutes.

Running his strong fingers through his blonde locks to shake out the sawdust, he opened the door of the converted barn that served as his workshop and stepped out into a broad swath of untended field. Behind the barn lay a fenced-off area of fifty culti-vated acres, owned by his uncle and aunt and farmed by a tenant. Ahead, a gentle slope rose up to the main house, a Tudor-era mansion now gone to seed. His aunt and uncle lived in one half of one floor, the rest of the mansion an echoing ruin they did their best to keep from falling down. The gardener's cottage, a little thatched-roof structure that looked more suitable for a hobbit, sat to one side and was Lucas's home.

He headed up the slope, already hearing the distant sound of the kettle Aunt Mary had put on.

A burly man in his sixties came around the corner of the house, waving with a hand encased in soiled gardening gloves. Uncle Philip, just coming back from working on the vegetable patch that provided much of their food.

A series of caws and the snap of wings made

Lucas turn around. A murder of crows rose from a large oak tree on the border between the farmland and the private land, spun in a tight circle, and shot off to the southeast.

Lucas felt prickles all along his skin. Crows did not rise from trees like that, and they did not fly in formation like that.

He watched them go, dwindling into the distance until they looked like a black bullet shooting straight for... something.

Lucas closed his eyes and let out a slow breath, opening his palms in the direction the crows had flown and spreading his arms.

He felt it—a low, crackling pulse like the static electricity of an approaching storm, but far deeper, far more powerful.

And then it was gone.

Lucas opened his eyes and stood for a moment longer. Nothing.

He turned and went up to the house.

He walked through a front hall adorned with oil paintings of landscapes and a few portraits of his ancestors, past a homey living room with overstuffed chairs, a huge Victorian sofa he really needed to reupholster someday, and floor-to-ceiling bookshelves, and down a short hallway following the sweet smells of tea and scones to the kitchen.

Aunt Mary looked up from the counter where she arranged scones on a plate, lines of concern creasing her face underneath her graying bun.

"What was that?" she asked.

"Crows making a tight twist as they rose and flying in close formation to the southeast."

"We'll look it up after tea," Aunt Mary said as she brought the plate of scones through the kitchen to the little back room they had converted to a dining room. The grand dining room of the house, once used to entertain visiting dignitaries, was now a library for Aunt Mary's vast collection of books.

"The tomatoes are coming along nicely," Uncle Philip said, grabbing a scone before Aunt Mary even got a chance to set the plate on the table.

"Manners, Philip," she said in a voice that showed she had given up trying to refine him long ago and loved him anyway.

Lucas and Aunt Mary sat. For a moment they didn't move, staring at their food in silence. Even Uncle Philip stopped chewing.

It was their version of grace. A moment's silence in gratitude for the bounty of the earth and the subtle powers that resonated through the seasons, giving life to the world.

At least that was what it meant for two at the table. Lucas knew Uncle Philip was only playing along. Being married to a witch, he believed in and appreciated these things, but he did not feel them in his soul. But Uncle Philip had worked for the Red Cross in some of the worst warzones and famines. His gratitude for a hot meal in a warm house came from a different source and was as deep or deeper than Lucas's or Aunt Mary's.

"How's the chair coming along?" Uncle Philip asked.

"Just about done. Next I'm doing a couple of picture frames for the National Gallery."

"So young and already found your calling," his uncle said with a smile. "You should be grateful. It took me years to find my way."

They had their tea, talking about commonplace things such as how the sheep were doing and the faucet that needed fixing in the downstairs bathroom. Once they were done, and Uncle Philip had put on his boots and gone to check on the sheep in the back field, Aunt Mary and Lucas did the dishes and went to the library.

The former dining room was a cavernous place,

still decorated with the swords and old banners of its original owners. They made a fitting backdrop to one of the best private magical libraries in the country.

Shelves of dark oak lined all the walls, and a standalone bookshelf ran down the center. At one end of the room, in front of the window, sat a Georgian-style table made by Lucas's own hands. Next to that stood a shelf piled with rolled-up maps. They walked over to it.

"Show me the direction the crows flew," Aunt Mary said.

He pointed unerringly in the exact direction they had taken. Lucas Lancaster had never been lost in his life. At least not physically.

Aunt Mary took out a compass and checked the direction of Lucas's finger. Then she pulled out a map of Oxfordshire.

"Such a tight circle as you described means that it's close," she said. "We want a detailed map for this. You said they rose from the boundary oak?"

"Yes, and straight as an arrow along the ley line."

"How high did they rise before leveling out?"

"I'd say sixty feet."

Aunt Mary cocked an eyebrow. "So quite close, then."

She unfolded the large map and weighed down

each corner with a small piece of jasper. The map was a standard Ordnance Survey map of Oxfordshire at the 1:25000 scale, a highly detailed map produced by the government that showed roads, buildings, copses, and most importantly, historic and ancient sites.

The entire map was crisscrossed with thin lines made with a fine pen. Aunt Mary had added those. They were ley lines, lines of power along the earth that the ancients had tapped into by building roads and religious centers.

One line passed right through their house. Aunt Mary said a stone circle lay there once, long ago. That circle was destroyed in Anglo-Saxon times to build a church, which had later decayed and been replaced with a medieval manor before it in turn got replaced in the Tudor period with the present house. The foundation contained large granite blocks from the medieval structure, and Aunt Mary believed the cellar dated to the Middle Ages as well and was really an expansion of the original church crypt. No trace of the stone circle existed. The early Christians would have obliterated that when they made the church. How Aunt Mary could know about it was something Lucas took on faith. Aunt Mary knew a lot of things other people didn't.

Aunt Mary's finger traced the line on the map as it passed across their property, right through the boundary oak, and then straight across the countryside, intersecting with an Iron Age hill fort, a stretch of old Roman road later used in the days of coach and fours, and two Neolithic standing stones spaced five miles apart before intersecting with another ley line at the King Stone. The other ley line cut through the middle of the King's Men and the Whispering Knights. Both lines continued across the country, indeed around the world, but Aunt Mary's finger had stopped.

"It's here," she said, tapping her finger on the King Stone. "Yesterday was the Feast of Saint Barnabas. Pity you were down in London yesterday. The crows would have given you quite a show otherwise."

"Did you see anything?" Lucas asked.

Aunt Mary gave an annoyed sigh. "It's passed on, Lucas. Accept it." In a softer tone, she continued. "I felt it, though. That never goes away."

"The radio said there's an archaeological excavation going on there."

"That wouldn't have caused this."

"So, what should I do?" Lucas asked, dreading the answer he knew would come.

"Go down there and take a look." Her words came out as an order, not a suggestion.

"Will you come?" Lucas's voice took on an adolescent whine that annoyed and embarrassed him. He couldn't help it, though.

"You were summoned," Aunt Mary replied. "Not I."

3

DELLA ARRIVED at the excavation site the next morning, unsure what to do. She was pretty sure her professor hadn't spotted her spying on whatever weird ritual had been going on the previous night.

Dr. Olding was there first, as usual, and was already setting up the theodolite to do some surveying.

"Hey, Della," she said. "We're expanding the grid a bit to the north. Once you clear out your square, we'll give you a new one."

"Sounds good," she said, searching her professor's face for any hint of suspicion. She saw none.

Della walked to the Oxford University van as it pulled up, whereupon she helped Evelyn and Donald, another graduate student, unload the tools, buckets, and piles of plastic bags that they would soon fill with bits of the past. Then she joined them in clearing off the tarps as the rest of the graduate students, undergraduates, and volunteers trickled in.

Usually this bit of exercise before starting the meticulous work of excavation exhilarated her, getting her juices flowing before kicking her mind into gear. Now her movements were clumsy and hesitant as her mind whirled. She looked around, trying to see if there was anything different about the site or the stones, and saw nothing.

So, what had Dr. Olding and those people been doing out here? It had seemed like some religious ritual.

"Della, could you come over here, please?" Dr. Olding said.

Feeling like a chastened school kid being sent to the principal's office, she obeyed.

Her professor held out a map of the site, showing the squares that had been excavated. She pointed to a cluster of marks indicating funerary urns.

"I say we follow this cluster, eh? How about two squares here and here. And I think another two squares over here where we found that dense flint scatter. I'd like to see if there was some sort of workshop."

"All right," Della said. Because she was her most promising student, Dr. Olding often brought her into the decision making. It wasn't so much that Dr. Olding needed her input, but the older archaeologist wanted to teach her student about the process of planning a dig.

Della had always felt grateful for this obvious sign of appreciation. She felt doubly so today because it appeared she had snuck away from the site last night without being noticed.

And then Winston showed up.

He walked right up to them, his thick glasses flashing in the sun.

"D-did you find your phone?" he asked. Dr. Olding glanced first at him, then at Della.

Della's heart leapt.

"Yes," she said quickly. "I had left it in my car."

"Oh," Winston said, confused. "I-I thought you—"

"Yes, but really it was in my car. I'm very absent-minded. Always have been."

Winston wandered off. Della relaxed. She got back to planning the dig with her professor, hoping the older woman couldn't hear the thudding of her heart.

The rest of the day passed quietly, at least as far

as everyone else was concerned. Della kept turning over the previous night's events in her mind, and try as she might, she couldn't reconcile the chanting woman in robes she saw with the practical, reticent professor she knew.

She got down to the depth that Dr. Olding asked, cutting through the soil quickly because there was little to find, just as she predicted. Angus, manning the sift, plucked out a few stray flints and tiny pieces of pottery, but nothing else.

At lunch break everyone got their sandwiches and thermoses and sat in small groups under the shade of the nearby trees. Della rushed through her meal and got up, heading over to the King Stone.

It stood out of sight from the excavation past some trees, although a couple of the vehicles were parked within view. To mask her intent, Della pulled out her phone. She had been taking photos of ancient sites for her Instagram feed. Several of her colleagues followed her account.

She circled slowly around the jagged stone, looking for anything unusual. She didn't see any marks on the pitted, lichen-encrusted surface, and she saw nothing in the grass except a couple of old cigarette butts dropped by careless visitors. She certainly didn't find any burn marks to explain that glow she saw as she had hurried away. They must have made that with artificial light.

But why? Why were they gathering around the old stone at all?

Of course Della had heard of the neo-pagan community, those modern-day nature-worshippers who tried to reinvent the old pre-Christian religions. She had even met a few. Archaeology conferences always attracted some eccentric hangers-on, and neo-pagans made up a large percentage of them. She had been roped into conversations a couple of times and was not impressed. They were generally well-read, and certainly visited a lot of historic sites, but their interpretations of ancient cultures were way off base. They tended to romanticize the pre-industrial past based on their own sappy ideals rather than any sort of evidence. They were sort of like American hippies with more books and less weed.

Dr. Olding didn't fit the profile. She was too serious to be a neo-pagan, too scientific. She was practical, hardworking, and logical. That was why she got along with Della so well.

"What are you looking for?"

Della almost jumped out of her skin. She spun and saw Dr. Olding standing a few paces away. Her face was an impassive mask, but Della swore she saw a glint of suspicion in her eyes.

"Oh, just annoyed that people throw cigarette butts here," she said as an explanation for why she had looked at the ground. "I was taking some pictures for Instagram. What do you think of this one?"

She held up the phone to show a photo of the King Stone, grateful that she had had the foresight to take some photos.

"Should be a hit," Dr. Olding said without enthusiasm. She had no time for or interest in social media. "You done with square seven?"

"I need another half hour after lunch to finish things up."

"That's fine. After that, break ground on square twenty-two. Winston has already pegged it out."

Dr. Olding turned as if to walk away and paused for a second. Della fell in with her, and they walked back to the site together. Neither said a word.

In the afternoon, Della hunkered down and focused on her work. That was a close call, and she didn't want to arouse any more suspicion than she already had. She tensed every time she saw her professor talking with Winston and hoped her classmate didn't mention where she had told him she had left her mobile phone.

She didn't know why she felt so paranoid about it. So, Dr. Olding was in some weird cult. So what? They hadn't damaged the stones or stolen anything as far as she could see, and it wasn't like they were sacrificing puppies or anything. Still, there was something unsettling about the ritual, and not just the fact that strangers in robes were chanting incantations under a full moon. It was something about their faces. They looked malicious, twisted. Especially that middle-aged man who had acted as their leader.

Della got to work and tried to convince herself she was overreacting.

Usually, breaking ground on a new square thrilled her. Now it just served as a distraction from her confused thoughts. She used a small spade to break through the topsoil. Angus sifted it and jokingly handed her an old beer can and a penny from 1978. Once she cleared off the topsoil, she got down to work on the interesting parts. The rule in archaeology was the farther you dug down, the earlier the material would be. The Bronze Age layer was a good thirty-five centimeters down. That was a lot of meticulous scraping with a trowel, even given that ten centimeters of topsoil had been taken off with a spade. If there was a funerary urn here—and given the cluster of urns in neighboring squares, there probably was at least one—she wouldn't get to it today or probably even tomorrow.

That didn't mean she wouldn't find anything interesting, though.

In fact, she found something within the first hour.

Della was scraping along with her trowel when she heard and felt the telltale rasp of metal on metal.

She set the trowel aside and picked up a wide paintbrush. With this she dusted away the earth and took in a sharp intake of breath.

It was a brooch, a beautiful silver brooch, about eight centimeters in diameter, and the pin, which often broke off such artifacts, was still intact. The silver was too encrusted with dirt for her to make out much of the design, but it looked compLucas. A work of art.

"Hey everyone, look at this!"

Angus and Hannah came over.

"Lucky," Hannah said, placing a ruler next to it and snapping a picture. She was the dig photographer and had remarkably steady hands, considering her nightly intake of alcohol.

Winston showed up and peered at it through his thick glasses.

"Hard to tell, b-b-but the style looks R-Renaissance," he said.

"Considering how close to the surface it is, I'd say you're right," Della agreed. "I'd better tag and bag it."

"I'll do it," Dr. Olding said, striding over.

She bent over the artifact, shouldering Della out of the way.

"This is very interesting," she murmured. "Very interesting indeed."

With brisk efficiency, Dr. Olding wrote the information on the bag and carefully lifted the brooch from the soil and put it inside.

"Keep going down and see if there are any associated finds," she told Della.

Della did as she was told, eager to find more. Dr. Olding remained by her side, holding the bag with the brooch inside. In the excitement of the moment, Della forgot about the weird scene she had witnessed the night before and Dr. Olding's uncharacteristic rudeness in pushing her aside to look at the brooch.

Excitement didn't make her sloppy, however. She scraped a bit more of the soil away and brushed it smooth in order to see the context better.

Taking care paid off. Now that she could see the soil clearly instead of as a disturbed mess, she noticed that the brooch had lain in a small, circular area of darker soil.

A pit. Common enough in archaeology. The darker soil came from a pit being excavated and put back into the hole to fill it. Because it was looser for a time after refilling, it attracted more moisture and organic matter and ended up darker than the surrounding soil, remaining so even centuries later. Pits were found in campfires, rubbish tips, and hoards.

The brooch was buried deliberately.

"Why would someone bury something so nice?" Hannah asked. No one present needed to have the significance of the soil marking explained to them.

"To hide it from looters, perhaps. Maybe it dates to the English Civil War," Dr. Olding said.

"L-looked older than that," Winston said.

"And there's no evidence of a pot or a bag like people usually use when putting something in a hoard," Hannah said.

"Sometimes archaeology doesn't give up all the answers," Dr. Olding said. "Winston, get back to your square. Angus, there's some more soil for you to sift. Hannah, take some general pictures of the excavation."

Everyone moved off. Della got back to work, measuring the dimensions of the pit and drawing them on her map of the square. Her professor stayed close.

Della didn't get to scrape down much further before being interrupted.

"We got a visitor," Angus said from his place at the sift.

Della looked up and saw a stranger standing at the edge of the excavation, a young man about her age. He had curly blonde hair and was tall and fit. Della thought him handsome and then immediately felt bad. She already had a nice boyfriend in Sebastian, and girls like her weren't exactly stud magnets. Her high school years were four years of awkward loneliness as far as boys were concerned. Her undergraduate years at the University of Pennsylvania weren't much better.

"Can I help you?" Dr. Olding asked, heading over to him, still holding the bag with the brooch.

They got visitors sometimes. As long as they stayed out of the excavation and didn't pester the archaeologists with too many questions, nobody minded.

The young man flashed a grin. "Oh, I was passing by, and I wanted to see what you were up to. I heard about your excavation on the radio."

"Um, yes. We're exploring the context of the megalithic remains here. Currently we're excavating a Bronze Age cemetery."

"Oh, that's interesting, I—"

"We're really quite busy, as you can see."

The stranger's gaze went down to the bag in her hand.

"Is that some sort of jewelry from that time?"

Dr. Olding pulled away a little. "No. It's from a … later period."

Della watched while the others got back to work. Her professor, while not the best spokesperson at handling the public, was usually politer than this.

Silence hung in the air between them for a long moment.

The young man grinned again. "Well, if you're busy, I guess I should leave you to it. Mind if I stay and watch for a bit?"

"Not at all," Dr. Olding said in a less than convincing manner. "Just please don't come into the excavation area."

"Oh, I won't get in your way. Is it all right to take a look at the stones as well?"

"Certainly," Dr. Olding said, already moving away.

Della got back to work. Her professor hovered close to her square for another hour until it became clear that no artifacts were associated with the brooch. Della scraped down the square until the little pit that had held the brooch disappeared. Then Dr. Olding left to take care of other matters.

The stranger lingered for a while, Della stealing glances of him, before he wandered off to look at the stones. Then he returned, stared at the excavation for a while longer, and got in his car and left.

Della watched him go.

4

"WELL, THAT WAS INTERESTING," Lucas said.

He and Aunt Mary sat drinking tea in the library. The books towered over them. The smell of old paper competed with the delicate scent of chamomile.

"How did it go?" Aunt Mary asked. "You came back rather quickly."

"I didn't get a chance to linger. The head of the excavation came up to me as soon as I arrived and told me not to come on the site."

"That's perfectly reasonable. It's delicate work they're doing."

"Her tone wasn't reasonable. I've been to loads of archaeological sites, you know how it's an interest of mine. People are generally quite nice. This Dr.

Olding told me they were excavating a Bronze Age cemetery and then sent me packing."

"At least she told you her name. That might help us a bit."

"Oh, I had to find that out myself. I knew it was an Oxford University project. It didn't take long searching through the faculty website before I found her photo. I did find out a little more, at least I think I did."

"Really?" Aunt Mary said, sipping her tea.

"A brooch. They had found a brooch, and quite recently, I believe, because it still had dirt clinging to it and Dr. Olding was holding the artifact bag. I got a rather queer feeling from it."

Aunt Mary leaned forward. "How so?"

"At first I didn't notice it coming from anywhere particular. I walked onto the site and felt a strange tingling feeling all over me. It grew as she approached, and I realized it came from the brooch itself. Later I felt it again when I touched the King Stone."

"Did you feel it anywhere else?"

"No. I went to the Whispering Knights and the King's Men, touching every stone. Nothing. I did have a general sense of oddness the entire time I was on the site, however. The tingling came only from the brooch and the King Stone."

Aunt Mary smiled. "You get more sensitive by the year."

"I thought I was more sensitive as a child," Lucas grumbled. "Or was that just hysteria?"

Aunt Mary's face darkened. "That was different. You had magic forced on you and a trauma that would scar any child. But don't say 'hysteria.' Outmoded psychological terms have no place in any discussion of magic."

"A psychologist might have done me some good."

Aunt Mary sighed and looked at him with loving, sad eyes. Lucas turned away.

It was the old argument, the one that never got resolved. When Lucas's parents got taken, Aunt Mary and Uncle Philip became his guardians.

And guard him they did. They kept the press at arm's length and avoided social workers and child psychologists as much as possible.

Lucas understood why. The normal world would not have understood what he had seen. The normal world would have called him mad. But he wished he could have had a bit more of the normal world. He might have turned out a bit more normal himself.

Maybe even happy.

Aunt Mary broke the silence. "So, what did this brooch look like?"

Lucas shrugged. "Couldn't really say. I only saw it for a moment before she put it behind her back. Circular, about seven or eight centimeters in diameter with a pin. It looked to be of silver, but it was still so dirty I couldn't see anything besides that."

"And you felt power emanating from it."

Lucas shrugged and took a sip of his tea. "I don't know what I felt."

"Yes, you do, Lucas. Stop fighting it. This could be significant. Think of the timing. You said it was covered with dirt. An archaeologist would have cleaned such a find fairly promptly. That means it was discovered shortly before you showed up. Synchronicity is already at work here."

"Or sheer coincidence."

"Don't pretend you don't believe in these things when I know you do," Aunt Mary said, becoming a bit cross. "Practitioners of the Craft have often imbued brooches with great power."

"Yes, Auntie, I've read Budge's *Amulets and Superstitions*."

"You need to read more deeply than that old primer. Here's a book that I think might help."

She lifted her rotund frame out of her armchair

and walked to a shelf, unerringly picking out the correct volume without having to look. Lucas smiled. Aunt Mary knew her library so well she could find books with the lights off. The old witch could probably read them with the lights off too.

She returned with a leather-bound volume titled *Magical Amulets of Medieval and Renaissance Britain* in gold lettering. No author byline appeared on the cover. When Lucas opened it up, he found no byline or publisher on the title page, just the publication date—1895. Most likely it was privately published by some Victorian practitioner. Precious few publishers would touch such a subject back then.

For this was no historical treatise. This was a how-to guide. Lucas flipped through it and saw incantations, instructions for creating magical amulets, and discussions of some of the great magical pieces of jewelry of the past. All of it was lavishly illustrated with detailed engravings.

"This must be a rare tome," Lucas said. "And worth a fortune. Let's sell it and fix the leaky roof in the attic."

"Knowledge has no price."

"Rising damp has a high one."

"Stop talking like your uncle."

Lucas laughed. Uncle Philip was the practical one while Aunt Mary spent most of her time in the hidden world. Lucas tried to straddle the line between them, trying to keep the house together while maintaining the original reason for its existence.

"It does look interesting," Lucas admitted. "At four hundred fifty pages, it's going to take some time, since you're also having me read *The Lesser Key of Solomon* and that biography of John Dee."

"Make this a priority. We need to identify that brooch if we want to understand what's going on here."

"Auntie, I barely glimpsed it."

"You'll have to get a closer look somehow."

"And how do I manage that? Break into the lab?"

Aunt Mary's face hardened. "If you have to. This is important."

"Bloody hell," Lucas muttered. Aunt Mary, like most practitioners of the Craft, respected human law as long as it didn't interfere with the higher laws of nature and the balance of cosmological forces. That was all well and good if you were puttering around your study or casting hexes on unappealing politicians, but no amount of magic would help you if the police came knocking.

"Take a look through this and ask me any questions you might have. Then think of a way to get back on that excavation."

"Oh, very well," Lucas said. "But I can't spend the entire day reading. Those chairs want finishing, and we need the money."

His aunt and uncle lived off the interest on an inheritance plus Uncle Philip's savings from his career as a physician. They also had the sheep and the rents from the land. That was barely enough to keep the house together. Old stately manors were incredibly expensive to maintain and came with ruinous property taxes, which was why so many had become hotels or empty ruins. Lucas's income made the difference between essential repairs and slow decay.

At times Lucas wanted to suggest leaving the place, selling it and cutting their losses, but it had been in the family for four generations, and power rested here. Aunt Mary's great-great-grandfather had purchased it from another family of witches who had decided to up stakes and move to America. Now they ran one of the largest covens in New England.

And he knew his aunt and uncle would never leave. They were too tied to the land, each in their own way.

After a bit of work in the woodshop finishing up the furniture, he settled down to the book Aunt Mary had lent him.

The ponderous initial essay taught him much he didn't know about the general use of amulets in magical ritual. After that he started flipping through the pages, looking for rituals and their associated amulets that were in any way linked with ancient sites.

He found several. Some of the older ones were meant to summon devils. Lucas smiled. Much superstition existed in magic, and it took a seasoned witch or wizard to tease out truth from fact. Devils didn't exist. At least not in the hidden world. The powers of dark and light were much subtler than that.

The rituals from the later Renaissance held more interest, especially those that tapped into the power of ley lines. The ancients had known all about these alignments of earth power, but much of the knowledge was lost with the decline of the Roman Empire and the ensuing Burning Times, when the early Christians systematically wiped out practitioners of the Craft and their accumulated knowledge. So much had been lost that a woman as wise as Aunt Mary would have been barely above novice level two thousand years ago.

Most rituals involving ley lines, he already knew, took three days to perform, usually the day before, during, and after the full moon, when the moon was at its strongest.

That meant he had already missed the first two nights of the ritual. What that ritual might be, he had no clear idea. The books showed him several brooches that could be like the one he had glimpsed. Too many. He couldn't narrow the ritual down. It might be for healing, knowledge, a simple act of worship, or something more malevolent.

One thing was for certain. He'd have to go back to the Rollright Stones tonight and see what sort of ritual they conducted. When he saw their organization and heard their incantations, he would be much surer of their purpose.

There was no other way.

He closed the book and covered his eyes with a trembling hand.

5

DELLA DIALED her boyfriend's number as she drove home from the dig that night. She needed some downtime.

Sebastian picked up after the third ring.

"Hello, darling. I was hoping you would ring."

Della smiled as she heard Sebastian's suave voice.

"I didn't ring, I called. Why do you English speak in such a silly way?"

"We speak proper Queen's English. 'Ring' is the proper term."

"The telephone was invented by an American, so we get to call it what we like."

"Actually, Alexander Graham Bell stole much of his work from the Italian Antonio Meucci, who made the first working telephone in 1860, sixteen years before Bell made his famous call."

"I bet you won a pub quiz with that useless bit of trivia," Della said, rolling her eyes.

"No, but I did win a pub quiz for knowing who was the first person to cross Greenland on skis."

"And who was that?"

"Fridtjof Nansen, of course."

"Of course. Stop pontificating and come over to my apartment. I'll cook you dinner, and you'll give me one of your famous back rubs."

"It's a deal. But I won't come over to your apartment, I'll come over to your flat."

"How do you say 'wiseass' in the Queen's English?"

"There's no direct translation. We usually say something wittily demeaning about Europeans."

"Just get over to my place. And bring some wine."

"Oh dear. Bad day in the sandbox?"

"You don't know the half of it."

Della hung up and drove to her place just off Iffley Road, one of the streets that ran out of Oxford and had a large student population. It was close enough to bicycle into campus or take the bus when England experienced one of its regular downpours.

Once, the previous autumn, it had drizzled for two weeks straight. Good thing she didn't get Seasonal Affective Disorder.

Her apartment was one half of the top floor of a divided Victorian house. She shared the house with five other tenants and their various boyfriends, girl-friends, and visitors. The place was too noisy for her liking, but it was the best she could afford. Her parents were both academics back in New York, and sending her to Oxford stretched their finances to the limit. Working for Dr. Olding got her a tuition waiver and a bit of money. Even so, school fees, books, and the cost of living here were insane. Della already worked hard, and the knowledge of what her parents were sacrificing for her career pushed her even harder.

Della tromped upstairs, grateful she didn't have to deal with any of her rambunctious neighbors on the landing, and took a shower. Then she got to work cooking up some stir-fry. By the time Sebastian rang the bell, dinner was nearly ready.

She opened the door to the most handsome man she had ever dated, not that she had dated many. Sebastian was her height, just five foot nine, rather shorter than she preferred, but he made up for it in looks and style. The looks came in the form of a broad, open face, easy smile, glossy black hair, and soft brown eyes. His style showed in everything from the casual yet classy way he dressed to his speech and mannerisms.

And his taste in wine.

"Will an '89 Cabernet Sauvignon wipe the tears away?" he asked, proffering a bottle.

"It's Tuesday night. You really shouldn't be buying wine bottled before we were born."

"Would madam prefer some cheap plonk with a screw top bought at Tesco?"

"Madam would prefer a kiss," she replied, putting her arms around him.

Madam got one.

It was delicious and yet over too quickly. They went to the kitchen, where Sebastian opened the bottle while she finished up with the stir-fry.

Over dinner, Sebastian asked about her day. She told him all about the work and the discovery of the brooch and how they had found that the Bronze Age cemetery was much more extensive than they had realized at first. He listened with interest and then told her of his day as a graduate student in the classics department. Since classes were over for the term, and he had already returned from a brief research trip to some of the sites in Greece, he spent most of his time in the Bodleian Library studying ancient Greek texts.

"The weather is really too nice to be locked up in the library," he concluded. "We must escape over the weekend. Punting, perhaps?"

"I'm outside all day," Della said with a smile.

"Mucking about in the dirt getting human ashes under your fingernails does not compare to me punting you down the river with a bottle of bubbly on ice."

"You've convinced me. Do I get that back rub now?"

"Only once I've poured us each a second glass of wine."

That he did, while Della lay down face-first on the bed. Then Sebastian came into the room, they each took a sip of their wine, and he got to work with those wonderfully delicate and sensitive fingers.

The man could work miracles. Not only was she totally relaxed within five minutes, but she was ready to open up when he asked her what was wrong.

"And don't tell me nothing's wrong," he added. "I can tell that there is. You are not the kind of girl who drinks two glasses of wine on a Tuesday. If I'm not very much mistaken, I might even be able to coax you into a third."

"If I didn't have to get up at 5:30 tomorrow morning, you probably could," Della admitted.

"Stop dilly-dallying and tell me what's the matter."

As those fingers kneaded her back muscles from the nape of her neck to the base of her spine, she let it all out—forgetting her phone, seeing the strange figures doing some sort of ritual, the weird light, Dr. Olding acting rude to a visitor. It didn't take long to tell, but telling it sure felt good.

For a moment, Sebastian didn't speak. When he did, his tone grew more serious.

"Shall we go out there?"

Della turned around. "What?"

"Perhaps they're out there again."

"Why would they be?"

"How should I know? I don't dress up in robes and chant next to stone circles under the full moon. But there's a chance they might be there again. I say if you want to know what's going on, the best way is for us to go take a look. If there's no one there, we come back, drink some more wine, and go to bed. If there is, you might just stop your professor and her mates from doing something foolish."

"I think the foolish thing would be to go out there," Della objected.

"Aren't you the least bit curious?"

Della paused before answering. "Yes. Yes, I am."

"Let's go then."

They hopped in her boyfriend's car because Della didn't trust herself to drive. Sebastian, being English, could hold his wine far better than a bookish American. She'd never get used to how much they drank in this country.

They parked more than a mile from the site on a quiet back road. From there they walked. The moon, just past full, had risen in the east and cast a silvery sheen over the fields. The wind picked up, and the grass and wheat waved like a stormy sea. Other than a few farms, they saw no lights at all.

"Beware of big black dogs," Sebastian said.

Della gripped his hand tighter.

"Do the farmers let their dogs run free?"

"Oh no, I was talking about demon dogs. They're often seen on English roads at night. They portend the death of whoever meets them."

"Very funny. If you want to scare me, tell me the farmers let their actual dogs out. I don't believe in ghosts, human or canine."

"They aren't ghosts. They're demons."

"I don't believe in demons either, and neither do you."

"Oh, I was just trying to make you feel safer. It's better than telling you about the series of mauling attacks by stray dogs in rural Oxfordshire, isn't it?"

"Stop that right now."

"Spoilsport."

After a few minutes, Della asked in a quiet voice, "You were kidding about the dog attacks, weren't you?"

"Would you like me to be nice, or would you like me to lie?"

"I knew this was a bad idea."

"Please don't start screaming. The cultists might hear us and decide to perform some human sacrifice."

"Cut it out. And keep your voice down. We're almost there."

Della had instructed Sebastian to park in a spot from which they would approach the site from the same direction as she had before. They could use a row of trees on that side as cover, and it was close to the King Stone, allowing them to get a better look at what was going on.

At first they didn't see or hear anything, but as they drew closer they heard distant voices. Della and Sebastian slowed down, peering through the trees, trying to catch a glimpse of any light.

At last they did, but it seemed small and faint, and it winked out quickly.

And then Della understood. Some people were there, but they weren't at the King Stone. They were at either the stone circle called the King's Men or at the tomb called the Whispering Knights. Those were across a narrow lane and past another row of trees.

And right next to the excavation.

Della's heart flip-flopped. The previous night, she had investigated because she feared someone had been looting the site. Now they may very well be doing exactly that.

The couple crept through the trees, pausing every now and then to listen. The distant light winked in and out through the trees on the opposite side of the road, but they could see nothing more than that.

They could hear voices. Male and female. They weren't chanting, only speaking, and Della couldn't pick out the words.

Della and Sebastian stopped.

"Now what?" Sebastian whispered into her ear, so softly she could barely hear him.

She shrugged and pointed to him to say, *This was your idea.* He grinned and cocked his head in the direction of the voices.

Summoning her courage, she stepped forward. The area was clear between the trees and the road, with only the King Stone for cover.

She jogged to the King Stone and hid behind it, Sebastian right behind her. The soft earth kept their footsteps from making more than the slightest noise. Della cocked her ear. The voices continued as before. She and her boyfriend moved to the narrow, two-lane road. No cars were parked there. The cultists or pagans or whatever they were must have parked some distance away, probably so as not to attract attention.

"Ready?" Della whispered to Sebastian.

"Not entirely, no. Are you?"

"No."

"Let's go, then."

They hurried to the road, tiptoed across it, and came to the trees.

Here they stopped. The growth wasn't very thick, and they could already get a patchy view of what was happening beyond.

This night saw more attendees—about twenty men and women in robes. They were arranged in three groups. Four of them stood around the Whispering Knights, the cluster of upright stones that had once been capped and covered with earth to act as some ancient chief's resting place.

A dozen more stood within the stone circle of the King's Men.

Four more people stood at the excavation. The tarpaulin that protected the site during the night had been pulled back, and the four robed figures stood around one of the squares.

Della jerked with surprise as she realized it was her new square, the one where she had found the brooch. Dr. Olding was one of the four.

They stood one to each side. Slowly they raised their hands, a wordless intonation resonating from their throats. The robed figures at the two megalithic structures did the same. Della shivered at the alien sound they made.

Moonlight flashed off something metallic on Dr. Olding's robe. Della squinted. It must have been a trick of the light, but something on her chest seemed to glow softly, as if absorbing the moonlight and strengthening it.

Entranced, Della stepped forward, trying to get a better look at what her professor had on her robe. A remote corner of her mind told her she was getting dangerously close to exposing herself, but she felt drawn to the strange white glow.

Sebastian grabbed her arm and pulled her back into the shadows. She jerked her head and blinked as if suddenly being woken up.

Her boyfriend drew her back another couple of steps to get out of sight.

Too late.

"Who's there?" one of the cultists demanded, pointing right at them.

They all turned and looked.

"Stop right there!" shouted the older man who had led the previous night's incantation.

Della and Sebastian bolted in the direction of the King Stone.

"Get them!" the older man shouted.

Della yelped as a dark figure burst out of a thicket not far to their left. A young man ran parallel to them not ten meters away.

He glanced to his right and spotted them.

As the moonlight shone on his face, Della recognized him.

It was the guy who had visited the excavation earlier that day.

6

LUCAS DID NOT HAVE time to wonder why two other people were spying on Dr. Olding and her fellow sorcerers. He was too busy running.

For a minute they ran in parallel for the nearest cover—the line of trees beyond the King Stone.

They made it just as their pursuers burst from the undergrowth closer to the ritual site, but they did not make it in time to avoid being spotted.

"They went that way!" one of the robed figures shouted.

Lucas veered toward the young couple.

"Which way is your car?" he asked.

The girl pointed in the opposite direction of where Lucas had parked. At that moment he recognized her as one of the archaeology students. She had stared at him while he spoke with Dr. Olding.

What was she doing here?

"Run for it," he instructed. "I'll distract them."

They split up, skirting the edge of the tree line. The shouts of their pursuers drew closer. Lucas pulled an electric torch out of his pocket and turned it on. The beam lit his way and gave away his position.

An instant later, someone shouted. "There!"

A triumphant roar rose from the crowd as they all moved in his direction.

Nice job, Lucas old boy, he thought. *You've saved the lady and her friend. Now find a way to save yourself.*

Turning off the torch and running as fast as he could seemed the best way—in fact, the only way.

Lucas angled to the right, away from the trees, to cut across an open field. Beyond stood a low stone wall about waist high. On the other side was a field of grain and a copse in the distance. If he could make that, he might be able to shake them.

Just then, the men and women in robes came out of the trees.

"Now we have him!"

"Where's the other one? There were two of them!"

"Grab him, and we'll make him tell."

Oh wonderful. They saw them and not you. This is what being chivalrous brings you.

Lucas hopped over the wall, then stumbled into a drainage ditch on the opposite side. He hissed in pain as his ankle twisted.

He stood, pain lancing through his ankle. His pursuers charged at him across the field, spreading out, the younger and faster ones in front, the older ones lagging behind, but all coming for him.

He got on one leg, rubbed his ankle, turned it a little to check the sprain wasn't too bad, and then bolted across the field of grain.

The summer had been dry, so the grain only reached his waist, not enough to hide him but enough to keep him from seeing where he was putting his feet. The pain in his ankle wasn't too bad, but if he twisted it again on the uncertain footing of this plowed field, he knew he wouldn't be able to get up again.

And judging by the sounds behind him, the fastest of his pursuers were gaining on him.

He made it to the copse without falling and then plunged into the shadows. At first the relief of having some cover overrode common sense, and he didn't slow down, but a few branches scraping against his face and a stumble over a root woke him up.

He forced himself to stop. He was in near darkness. The moonlit sky shone distant and dim through the canopy of leaves, little of its light filtering down to where he stood. He could only vaguely make out the trees around him.

Lucas had studied the area on Google Earth before coming here and remembered that this copse was fairly large, at least a few acres. To one side ran another country road that would lead him, after a kilometer, to an intersection with another little road. A hundred meters on that other road would take him to his car.

Sadly, the terrain was more or less open between the copse and his car. Some bushes, a tree or two, and not much more.

He'd have to worry about that part of his escape later, because just then he heard the sound of snapping branches and tearing leaves as several people entered the copse.

The sound quickly stopped.

"Where is he? I can't see a bloody thing," one of them whispered. Lucas tensed to hear how close the man sounded. Lucas hadn't run into the copse as far as he thought he had.

"You have a torch?"

"No."

Louder. "Anyone got a torch?"

More sounds of running feet.

"No," a breathless voice said.

A feminine voice carrying a sense of authority said, "You, go back and get as many torches as you can. There's some in the bags. The rest of you, spread out around the edge of this copse. He can't have passed through. We'll trap him and flush him out."

Lucas thought he recognized the voice of the excavation director, Dr. Olding.

Lovely that you told me your plan, duckie, Lucas thought. *Now if I could only think of a way to stymie it.*

He needed to get through the copse and onto that road before they surrounded his hiding place. Lucas was fairly sure he knew the right way to go and almost certain he couldn't go that way without making a terrible racket.

Taking a few experimental steps, he found he didn't make too much noise if he walked slowly. The people hunting him masked the sound of his movement as they shouted instructions to one another. He could hear them spreading out around his hiding place and heard more coming up to join them.

He crept deeper into the copse, knowing he was going too slowly. That fellow who had gone to fetch some torches was no doubt running for all he was worth, as were the men and women creating a ring around the cluster of trees. Lucas could tell he wouldn't make the opposite side in time. He had to pick up the pace.

He did and in the process made a huge amount of noise.

"Shh, listen! He's moving around in there."

Lucas tried to move more quietly. That worked for all of three steps until he snapped a twig underfoot.

This time no one spoke, although Lucas could hear the rustle of their robes and tread of their feet. They were listening, trying to gauge his location and move to where they thought he would emerge.

There was nothing he could do but oblige them. He moved through the thicket, wincing every time he rustled a bush or snapped a twig.

As the branches thinned ahead and a bit to his left, he paused and listened. The silence was deafening. The clearing was only a short run away, but he had the sickening suspicion that he had veered a bit too much to the left.

Only one way to find out. That chap with the torches would be along presently.

He rushed to the edge of the copse, lifting his legs high in the hope of not tripping on any hidden roots or stones.

That worked, almost.

He got right to the edge of underbrush before tripping ...

... and landing literally in the arms of a burly male in flowing white robes.

Lucas gave him an uppercut that he meant to land on the point of the jaw and knock the man out cold, but he fumbled it and only gave him a glancing blow to the ear.

That was enough to make the man cry out and stagger back a step.

Lucas's next punch landed square on his nose.

The fellow dropped. Very obliging of him. Woodworking and helping Uncle Philip in the fields had developed Lucas's muscle tone. He smiled. He'd have to boast about this later.

A sound to his right told him that there might not be a "later."

A woman stood not five paces away. She glared at him and hissed.

Actually *hissed.*

Lucas raised his fist.

"Don't make me act against my upbringing."

The woman backed off, looking appalled. Lucas felt a twinge of guilt, highly inappropriate considering the circumstances, and glanced around. The curve of the copse kept him out of view of any of the other worshippers.

"He's over here!" the woman shouted, continuing to retreat.

Once again chivalry has tripped you up, my man.

The road lay not far ahead. Lucas ran for it, trying to ignore the pain in his ankle.

He made it, hopped a low stone wall he hadn't seen on Google Earth, and got into the road.

"Get him!"

Several men and women came around both sides of the copse, heading straight for him. He crossed the road and hopped another stone wall into the field beyond.

Headlights appeared far down the road. The people hunting him paused. Lucas jumped back over the wall and onto the road.

The car drew closer, and the cultists backed away out of sight.

Lucas walked toward the approaching car, waving his hands over his head and exaggerating his limp.

Please don't be a lone woman too afraid to pick up a strange man after dark.

The car slowed, not that it had much choice with Lucas placing himself right in the middle of the road.

A window lowered.

"You all right?" a male voice asked.

Oh, thank the powers of the Earth.

"Um, no. I was out looking for a stray sheep and twisted my ankle. Can you drive me back to my house?"

There was a farmhouse not far from where Lucas had parked. He hoped the man wasn't a local and knew the residents.

"Sure. Hop in."

"You don't know what this means to me. Really, you don't."

TWO HOURS LATER, Lucas sat at home in front of the fireplace as a merry blaze crackled and warmed his foot, which was wrapped in a packet of ice and up on a stool. He sipped a cup of tea and looked pensively into the fire. Uncle Philip and Aunt Mary sat on the sofa nearby.

"This is serious," Aunt Mary said.

"I'm aware of that, Auntie. I was the one getting chased across the fields by a pack of ravening cultists."

"I mean the ritual. No doubt they returned and finished it once you were gone."

"Perhaps. That motorist who gave me a lift didn't spot them. As long as they didn't think we went to the police, they would have felt safe enough."

"Did you get a look at what the archaeologist was wearing? You said it glowed."

"All I saw was a glow, a silvery glow. I suppose I should have gone up and inspected her chest with a magnifying glass, but you raised me to respect the ladies."

"Don't talk back to your aunt," Uncle Philip said. "She's trying to help."

"I didn't get a clear view of what she was wearing. My impression is that it was some sort of brooch. Whether it was the same they dug up earlier today, I have no idea."

"Did you feel anything?" Aunt Mary asked.

"A vague tingling. I think they were just beginning the ritual. They hadn't started the words to the incantation when that archaeology student revealed herself."

"You need to find her," Uncle Philip said.

"I already have. Her photo is on the department website. She's a graduate student from America. Della Marshal. I searched around the Internet for more information. She has an Instagram account with photos of archaeological sites, and there are a few old newspaper articles where she's mentioned as being part of various excavations in the United States. That's all."

"Not much of a cyber footprint for someone your age," Uncle Philip observed.

"More than mine."

"You're a recluse who needs to stop puttering around old houses and make some more friends," his uncle said.

"Really? I thought my social life was radically improving. Just tonight, an entire cult was practically throwing themselves at me."

"Cheeky bastard," his uncle said with a laugh. "Want some whiskey?"

"That's the best idea I've heard all day. After

that I think I'll go to bed. My ankle hurts, and I have somewhere to go tomorrow."

"Where's that?" Aunt Mary asked.

"The archaeology department at the uni. I'm going to go have a chat with Della Marshal. The weather says it will rain buckets tomorrow, and so I suspect that's where she'll be."

7

DELLA DREADED GOING into the department the next morning. She woke up to the patter of rain on the window and a group text saying the dig was called off for the day. The sky was slate gray, and BBC Weather predicted rain for the next ten hours. When this happened, the volunteers got the day off, while the graduate students would put in a day's work at the laboratory.

"Don't go," Sebastian said as they still lay in bed.

"If I don't, they'll ask questions."

"What if it's a trap?"

"We always do this when it rains. Besides, I don't think they saw who I was."

"You don't know that."

"Look, I don't want to go either, but it's not like I

have a choice. She knows someone was spying on her. If she saw me, I'll have to face her sooner or later. If she didn't see me, she'll suspect it was me if I don't show up today. In any case, the lab is right on campus. She can't try anything there with all those people around."

Della got up to make breakfast.

"I'm coming with you," Sebastian said, following her. "Make up some excuse for my being there. And when your work day is over, I'll come pick you up."

Della kissed him. "You're a sweetheart."

Sebastian smiled. "I am, aren't I?"

Della's heart pounded, and sweat trickled down her back by the time she and Sebastian made it to the department, housed in a fine old Victorian building of red brick. Sebastian held her hand as they came in from the rain. They passed through the front hall, where a secretary was putting mail into the wooden mailboxes lining one wall. The middle-aged woman glanced at Sebastian and gave Della a smile that said, *Aren't you lucky?*

That made Della feel better. Yes, she was lucky to have such a handsome guy.

And damn lucky he was coming along to protect her.

They ascended the creaking stairs, Della

nodding to one of the senior professors who absent-mindedly nodded back. Professor Seton was well on the wrong side of eighty and yet still came into the office every day. He hadn't conducted an excavation or written a paper or taught a class in years, but here he was, his tie neatly tied, a sheaf of printouts under his arm. Della suspected he would be lost without an academic department to go to.

I suppose I'll be like that someday. It was not a cheery thought.

They reached the upper floor and walked in silence down the hall past office doors, most closed for summer. The faculty had spread to the far corners of the world to conduct excavations—Egypt, Vietnam, Crete, and places closer to home like Scotland and the Isle of Man. At the end of the hall, the door to the lab stood open. They could see Evelyn sitting at the end of a table, looking through a microscope.

Della hesitated, but Sebastian gently tugged her along.

They walked to the door. Evelyn looked up and said hi before focusing on the microscope again.

Della stepped into the lab, a large room with two long tables taking up much of the space. On the other end of the same table Evelyn was using,

Hannah had set up her photographic equipment and was taking pictures of various artifacts cleaned up by Nigel and Winston, who sat at the other table. Nigel was picking out dirt from a bone comb dating back to the Neolithic, while Winston glued together the broken pieces of a Bronze Age urn that had shattered at some time in antiquity.

The only person Della didn't see was Dr. Olding.

"Hello, everyone," she said, somewhat uncertainly, searching for anything unusual in their expressions.

"Oh hello, Della," Nigel said with a sly smile. "Sleep in today?"

Della blushed. Sebastian saved her by introducing himself.

"Nice meeting you, mate," Nigel said. "I'd like to say we've heard a lot about you, but actually we've heard nothing."

"Oh really?" Sebastian said, cocking an eyebrow at Della.

Della shifted on her feet. Being socially awkward made it difficult to talk about herself, and now she realized that except to Hannah, who had directly asked, she had never told any of these people she was dating someone.

"And who's this?" said Dr. Olding from behind her.

Della whirled around.

"Sebastian," she squeaked, turning around to look at her professor, who had just come in from the hall. "He wanted to see where I work."

Dr. Olding extended a hand to her boyfriend, who shook it. She gave him a flat smile.

"Pleased to meet you, Sebastian. By all means, come in and take a look."

Della and her boyfriend exchanged glances. If Dr. Olding suspected they had spied on her the previous night, she was a star actress. She seemed her normal self.

In a way, that actually disturbed Della even more. Perhaps they really had avoided being recognized. But Dr. Olding had been conducting some kind of ritual the previous night, then tried to hunt down some intruders and do God-knows-what to them.

And she didn't look ruffled at all.

How could someone lead such a radically double life and show no outward signs of it?

Della tried to focus on the conversation.

"I have some reports to write up," her professor said to Sebastian, "but let me give you a quick tour.

Evelyn here is looking at soil samples. She's doing her dissertation on paleoethnobotany. Do you know what that is?"

"The study of how ancient people used plants."

Dr. Olding gave another one of her flat smiles. "You've been dating Della for quite some time, I see. She's rubbing off on you. Yes, that's correct. Evelyn is studying these samples looking for seeds and pollen grains. They'll give us an insight into what sorts of plants were being used by the ancient cultures we're excavating."

"Interesting."

Evelyn looked up from her microscope and gave Sebastian a sultry smile. Sebastian gave her a curt nod in reply and moved on to where Hannah was making her photographs.

The only guy not to flirt with Evelyn is my boyfriend? Della thought. *Looks like I'm finally having a bit of luck with men.*

Della slunk over to her spot at the table, where lay a tray of flints she had been cataloging. Perhaps if she quietly got to work, she would escape her professor's notice.

Dr. Olding continued the tour. Sebastian chatted briefly with Hannah, then moved over to Nigel, who allowed him to put on some gloves and hold the bone comb.

"Gentlemen, if I drop this, Della is sure to break up with me. She likes French wine, classic film, and back rubs. Best of luck."

That got everyone giggling. Even Dr. Olding broke into something approaching a real smile.

After he set the comb down as gently as one would a newborn, he moved over to Winston.

"And who might you be, jigsaw man?"

"W-Winston. I'm putting together this p-pot."

"Very clumsy of them to break it. You just couldn't get good help in those days."

Sebastian and Winston started to have a conversation, and Della got to work, grateful for his presence. Sebastian was one of those people who could get along with anybody. Dr. Olding went and sat at a computer at the far side of the room.

After a time, Sebastian came over.

"I have to go," he said, looking at her with concern.

"It's all right," she replied. *I hope.*

"Ring me if you need to. I'll be in the Bodleian."

The library was only a short walk away. That made her feel better.

When he walked out the door, Della tensed, unsure what to expect, but Dr. Olding continued typing. She didn't rise from her computer for another hour and then only to bring Della some more artifacts to catalog.

Apparently, no one had recognized her the previous night.

That still didn't satisfy her curiosity about what the hell was going on.

When lunchtime came, Della headed out the door with a sigh of relief. She put on her raincoat, walked out the building, and pulled out her phone to text Sebastian.

"Excuse me," a male voice said behind her.

She turned and froze.

It was the young man from last night, the other person who had spied on Dr. Olding and her strange group. He wore a raincoat with the hood pulled close to hide his features, but he stood close enough to her for Della to see his face.

"I ... um ..." Della sputtered.

The man smiled. "Yes. Awkward. Is there somewhere we can chat? Preferably as far from the archaeology department as possible?"

"I was just going to call my boyfriend to meet him for lunch."

"I'm not trying to pull you. Magical rituals under

the full moon aren't the sorts of places where I tend to go to meet women."

Della supposed that was meant to be funny. This whole situation was too weird for her to laugh.

"I know a good place," she replied, putting her phone back in her pocket.

They started to walk. Della set a quick pace. The stranger seemed relieved to be getting out of the department's sight.

"Sorry for the cloak and dagger. I'm Lucas Lancaster."

"I'm Della Marshal. I guess you already know that."

"I looked you up on the departmental website. Google stalking, I know. Very passé. Under the circumstances I hope it's forgivable."

"You should meet my boyfriend. He has the same sense of humor."

"Would you mind terribly if you don't call him? What I have to tell you should probably reach as few ears as possible."

Suspicion rose within her. Quickly she decided that was the wrong reaction. This guy had distracted the cultists to let them escape.

Then she noticed that he limped.

"Did you get away all right?" she asked.

"A bit of trouble, but I made it in the end. I've been waiting outside the department for the past hour hoping you'd appear. It was a terrible risk—several of them know my face—but I needed to speak with you."

"I have some questions of my own. Let's wait until we have some privacy."

She led him to a pub called the Mason's Arms. Lucas laughed when he saw the sign.

"What's so funny?"

"Oh, just a little bit of synchronicity."

"You're an odd fellow."

"Oh no, they go to a different pub," Lucas said, chuckling.

"Could you let me in on the joke, please?"

Lucas cleared his throat. "Terribly sorry. Actually, none of this is funny. Why did you pick this particular place?"

"There's a private room where we can talk without being overheard."

The Mason's Arms was a strange little pub. The interior was divided up into several booths, each with its own wooden partitions. Some even had doors. Most could seat four to six people. One at the back seated only two. Sebastian had taken her here once and explained that this was a rare example of a preserved Victorian pub. Back then, little private cubicles called "snugs" were common in pubs. She felt guilty about leading this strange man, who acted stranger by the minute, to a spot where she had been brought on a date.

At the bar, Della ordered a Coke, and Lucas ordered a pint.

"It's a good painkiller," he explained to Della.

"Did they hurt you?"

"They certainly tried. No, I hurt myself running from them."

The pub didn't serve meals, so not many people were in there at this hour, just a few professional drinkers and a couple of students necking in one of the stalls.

Della blushed and led Lucas to the back, where there was a little stall with a door that closed.

She closed it, sat at the tiny table, and studied the man sitting across from her. He took a sip from his beer, his blue eyes never leaving her.

"All right," Della said. "You seem to know a lot more than I do. So, what's going on?"

8

LUCAS SIGHED. Where to begin? The girl was right. He did know a lot more than her, but that still amounted to precious little.

He studied the woman sitting across from him. She was a couple of years younger than he was, pretty, but had a bit of an uptight, businesslike air. Definitely a university scholar type. Lucas had never gone to uni. He had seen no need. All he wanted to do was tend sheep, manage the land, and make antique-style furniture better than practically anyone else in the country. Plus, he had found that many students with fistfuls of advanced degrees were far less educated than he was, especially in the sort of information that really made a difference in the world.

The kind of information he felt quite certain this graduate student in archaeology had never bothered to look up.

And now he had to teach her.

"Your professor is part of a magical group," he began.

"What, like a coven?"

Lucas inclined his head. "Not exactly. Covens are for witches, practitioners of Wicca. This is a different sort of magic."

"Druids? Alchemists?"

Her voice trailed off. Lucas got the sense that she had just reached the limits of her knowledge of the magical arts.

"No, this is Earth Magic."

"Dr. Olding isn't a hippie."

Lucas chuckled.

"Your American hippies don't worship anything but their own hedonism. This is a more serious enterprise."

Della cocked her head and studied him.

"You believe in this stuff, don't you?"

"I do, because unfortunately it's all too real." He raised a hand when he saw she was about to object. "I know you think it's all tosh, the intellectual equivalent to the Flat Earth movement, but I assure you it's quite powerful in its own subtle way. Now I'm not asking you to believe. Go on the assumption that it's all bollocks if you like, but realize that your professor and her cronies believe it's very much real, and are acting accordingly."

Della thought about this for a moment.

"All right," she said dubiously.

He took a breath and asked, "Have you heard of ley lines?"

Della rolled her eyes. "Oh, for God's sake!"

"I'm not saying you have to believe. The important thing is to understand that Dr. Olding does believe. If you were up against an Aztec priest who wanted to rip your heart out to appease the sun god, you wouldn't argue theology with him, would you? No, you'd run for dear life."

Della got a serious look on her face. "Are you saying these people are dangerous?"

Lucas met her eye. "Yes. Yes, they are. They're not going to hurt anyone who isn't standing in their way, at least not yet. But what they're planning could be extremely dangerous for many, many people."

"And what are they planning?"

Lucas took another sip of his pint to collect his thoughts.

"I'm not entirely sure. I didn't get to see enough

of the ritual to know precisely what they are trying to do, but it involves tapping into the Earth energy running through the ley lines. The King Stone is a nexus of two ley lines passing through the countryside, connecting ancient places of power."

Lucas could see he was losing her. Nevertheless, he went on.

"This group is obviously trying to use that power for its own purposes. Many magical societies and individuals do. Some perform rituals of healing. Others use the ley lines as a way to practice divination. The way they reacted to us, and the little of their ritual I saw, tells me they are up to no good."

"Oh, come on. Chanting some weird words around a prehistoric site isn't going to harm anyone. And yes, I get it. They think it will, but it won't. They reacted badly when we interrupted, and obviously my professor is a nutcase who is very good at pretending to be a normal person, but that doesn't mean they're actually going to hurt anybody. Magic isn't real, and casting spells doesn't do anything."

"But—"

"They didn't damage the site, and they didn't take anything, so why should I object? They're only dangerous if we bother them, so I'm going to leave them alone."

Della rose.

"They did take something," Lucas said.

That stopped her.

"What?"

"The Renaissance brooch you people dug up yesterday."

"And how do you know that?" she asked, sitting back down.

"Because Dr. Olding was wearing it last night."

Lucas didn't know that for certain. He wasn't even sure the brooch dated to the Renaissance. He was working on a hunch.

"You got close enough to see it?" she asked, her skepticism obvious in her tone.

You're a sharp one, Della Marshal, Lucas thought.

"No, but I am familiar with those sorts of items of power."

"Items of power?" More skepticism.

Lucas held up a hand. "Remember to think along their lines. I'm not asking you to believe. During the sixteenth to nineteenth centuries, there was a rise in Earth worship in the British Isles, people trying to regain the knowledge that had been lost during the oppression of the church. While the religious author-ities still burned and hanged so-called witches up to the end of the seventeenth century, the spread of the printing press and better communication with practitioners on the Continent meant that there was a freer exchange of information. Quite a lot of these rituals were conducted, and relatively few people involved were caught and tried for witchcraft, although sad to say, there were some lost to society's intolerance."

"I thought the people tried as witches were mostly social outcasts and the insane."

"Most were. Some were real followers of alternative faiths such as Earth Magic. Virtually none were what we today call witches, followers of Wicca."

"And how do you know all this?"

Lucas smiled. "I come from a long line of magicians. My family library is one of the best in the country."

He was losing her again. How does one talk to a skeptic about things they need to know but don't want to hear? He hurried to go on.

"So back to your brooch, and how I know Dr. Olding stole it. Who uncovered it? I mean, who actually dug it up?"

"I did."

Lucas blinked. Another synchronicity. His days were becoming full of them.

"It had been deliberately buried, hadn't it?" he asked.

Della's eyes widened. "How did you know that?"

"You found evidence that it had been deposited in a small pit. You saw a small circle of darker soil around the brooch. I'm familiar with archaeological techniques, you see. I've even volunteered on a few excavations."

A look of suspicion crossed her features. Lucas laughed.

"Don't worry. I didn't steal anything."

"Go on," she replied, treating him to a level gaze.

"One of the elements of many Renaissance rituals was to imbue an item with power by wearing it during a ritual and then burying it along a ley line. It would gain more power the longer it remained buried. Brooches or rings were common, because regular people would assume they were harmless pieces of jewelry."

"That's stupid. Wouldn't burying a piece of jewelry get it all rusted or tarnished? Why wouldn't they put it in a lead casket or something?"

"The brooch would be wrapped in magical herbs, which of course had long since rotted away by the time you made your discovery. The magic in the herbs would preserve the brooch."

Della treated him to a sarcastic smile. "Sorry, but the brooch was all dirty and tarnished when I pulled it out of the ground."

"Did you rub the dirt off and actually check it was tarnished?"

"No, that's a job to do at the lab."

"And what did you see at the lab?"

Della paused. "You know, we didn't work on the brooch at all this morning."

"A prize find, and that wasn't the first thing your professor wanted to work on?"

Her mouth hung open. "Hey, you're right. That is a bit odd. She didn't even mention it, and I was so nervous I didn't think to bring it up."

"Bring it up this afternoon and see what she says."

She cocked her head. "So, what's this magical brooch supposed to do?"

"I don't really know because I didn't get to see enough of their ritual. Most can be used for a number of purposes. The brooch is a storehouse of Earth energy that can then be used to feed back into the Earth current and bring forth the desired magical result. The longer the amulet is buried along a ley line, the more powerful it becomes. This one has been buried for centuries and thus would be extremely powerful."

Della's eyes had glazed over.

He took a gamble. "You saw it glow."

"I saw it catch the moonlight. I didn't see it glow."

Did he sense a note of uncertainty in her voice?

"And no doubt you felt drawn to it. I certainly did."

"Drawn to it? No."

The denial came too quickly. Silence hung in the air between them.

Della broke it first. "Look, thank you for helping me and my boyfriend get away. I think it's best if we just pretend it never happened. Okay, so Dr. Olding has some oddball beliefs, but she's still a professional archaeologist, and she's not going to do anything to harm the site."

"She would have done something to harm us if her goons had caught us."

Another silence. This time it was Lucas who broke it.

"Let me give you my number. I won't ask for yours. Go back to the lab and check on the brooch. If it's there safe and sound and looks like it's been in the ground for a few centuries, you can delete my number and pretend you never met me. If it's gone, or if it looks like it was made yesterday, give me a ring and we'll talk further."

Della hesitated.

"All right," she said at last.

He gave her his number, and she got up to leave.

"I really need to get something to eat," she said by way of an excuse.

"You do that. 'Chew it over,' as you Americans say."

She gave him a ghost of a smile. "Right."

"And please, let's keep this between ourselves. Your boyfriend knows too much already."

Della's brow furrowed. "Why shouldn't he know all of it?"

"For his own safety. I'm only telling you because you're on the excavation, and you're the one who found the brooch. You're linked to this. He's just an innocent bystander."

She stared at him for a moment and then turned to go.

"And Della ..."

She turned back to him.

"Do be careful."

9

DELLA WAS the last person to make it back to the lab. After leaving Lucas at the Mason's Arms, she had wandered aimlessly for a while amid the town's Gothic spires, ignoring the rain as her mind swirled with all the weird stuff she had just heard. Then she sat in a café eating some soup and a bun, Lucas's words running over and over in her mind.

It was all nonsense, of course, and yet Lucas had made a point. It didn't matter so much if all this Earth Magic wasn't true if Dr. Olding and her cult thought it was. They had chased after Lucas, Della, and Sebastian, and she shuddered to think what would have happened if any of them had been caught.

Too many things about that night disturbed her, too many unanswered questions.

The big one was what had happened to the brooch.

Lucas was right about that, at least. She should ask about it, because if Dr. Olding had stolen it, that would be a serious offense. Della told herself it would be perfectly natural for her to enquire about the best find she had made on the dig.

That didn't stop her heart from thudding in her chest as she entered the Archaeology Department.

Dr. Olding looked up from her desk as she came in.

"Ah, there you are. If you could finish those flints today, that would be great."

"I will. Then I can get to work on the brooch."

Dr. Olding's reply took a second longer to come than it should have.

"Oh, I sent it down to Imperial College to have their archaeometallurgy team clean it. They have better facilities than we do."

Della nodded and sat down, confused. Imperial College London did have an excellent archaeometallurgy lab staffed by experts in ancient metals, but so did Oxford. Dr. Olding had never sent anything down there before, as far as Della knew. Just last week Winston had uncovered a rare Anglo-Saxon *sceat*, a silver coin worth hundreds of pounds on the collector's market. That hadn't been sent to the lab at Imperial College or even Oxford. Dr. Olding had let Winston clean it, and he did a perfectly good job. Della could have done it too.

And there was that bronze arrowhead Nigel found. He had cleaned that up just this morning. There had never been any talk about sending that away to another lab.

She sat, staring at the tray of flints she had to record in the excavation files.

Della worked through the rest of the day on automatic pilot, feeling like a robot as her mind whirled with a hundred questions, none of them answerable.

That evening the rain still poured down as Della swung by her apartment to pick up her fencing gear. She had team practice that night. While she really didn't want to go, Della decided that it would be a good way to take her mind off things. Perhaps focusing on something else would clear her head and give her a new perspective.

That would sure be a help, because she had no idea whether she should call Lucas about the brooch or not.

Sebastian had texted her at lunchtime asking

how things were going, and she had told him that everything was fine and she would speak with him after practice. To her surprise, she found that she had no intention of telling him the bizarre conversation she had with Lucas. The guy had said that Sebastian would be safer not knowing with such conviction that it had shaken her. If there really was some danger here, it might be better holding off on telling Sebastian anything.

He texted her again asking if she wanted to meet. She sensed he was worried about her. Getting chased last night had probably rattled him as much as it had Della. She texted him back reassuring him that she was fine and saying that she really wanted to take her mind off things and relax that evening. She promised that they would get together the next day.

Della felt bad fobbing him off like that, but she needed some space.

But that's part of the problem, isn't it? she thought. *You've been making people give you space all your life.*

Sure, another part of her mind replied. *At least this time I have a damn good reason.*

Her fencing team met at the university gym, just off Iffley Road and within walking distance of her apartment.

For one of the richest universities in the world, Oxford didn't have much of a gym. The grounds were nice, a track and a couple of playing fields surrounded by trees, but the building itself was musty and in need of upkeep. The weight room smelled of sweat and old socks. She didn't even want to think about what the men's locker room smelled like. The women's locker room was bad enough. The building had a decent pool, though, a court that was used for basketball and various other games, and a few rooms for the sports clubs.

The fencing team met in one of these, a grim concrete rectangle of a room that left nothing pleasing for the eye.

Just as well, because in fencing, if you took your eye off your opponent for more than half a second, you were dead.

Having changed into her white padded fencing costume and carrying her epee and mask, she entered the room, nodded a greeting to her teammates and coach, and started to limber up.

Fencing had been her father's idea. In contrast to her younger brother Greg, who loved sports and had played rough and tumble with his dad since he was a toddler, Della had been withdrawn and bookish right from the start. Dad obviously missed having another kid to play catch and climb trees with and so came up with a sneaky plan. When Della reached age thirteen, an awkward age for any girl and twice as awkward for her, he noticed that she had taken an interest in the Middle Ages. Della devoured books on lords and ladies, castles and tournaments, and she read stacks of cheap fantasy novels.

So, when the next Olympics came around, her father sat her down, and together they watched the women's fencing competitions.

Della got hooked. There was a strange grace to the fencers' movements, a mixture of aggression and poise. It had hints of the medieval but took place in the modern day.

Even better, she would get to wear a mask to hide her zits and braces.

Dad signed her up the following week.

She turned out to be a natural. Hidden behind the screen of the fencing mask, her developing body swaddled in thick protection, Della was free of all her physical inhibitions, and her natural dexterity and timing came to the fore. She won her first medal at fourteen, her first state juniors' championship at sixteen.

Fencing had given her a base of self-confidence that carried her through university and into a graduate program. While it hadn't solved all her problems—she still got nervous with new people and in crowds—fencing had become an integral part of her life and her self-esteem.

It helped that she was still damn good at it after ten years, good enough to make it onto one of the best university teams in the country.

Only a few members of the team were there during the summer, most having gone off for holidays in summer villas in France or Spain. Fencing was a rich person's sport in England, and Della was the only fencer who came from a family who owned only one home. A couple of her teammates' parents even had titles.

She didn't care. Even though she was never invited to the parties, she didn't want to go to them anyway, and she made up for it by regularly beating her teammates in practice.

Which was what she proceeded to do again.

As an opponent she picked Amanda, a six-foot blonde with a little pointy upturned nose and an accent that oozed breeding and privilege. A cushy life didn't stop Amanda from having lightning reflexes and a clever technique. One should never underestimate Amanda.

They stood a few steps apart, saluted one

another with their epees, saluted their coach who was acting as referee, and got into the proper stance —legs apart, sword forward with the sword arm slightly bent, other arm up and back.

Della was known as the aggressive one. Once that mask went on, she transformed. She knew Amanda was banking on her attacking first and would parry her attack with a quick flick of her wrist and send in one of her famous ripostes. Blink and you miss it.

Blink and you lose.

So, Della hung back, taking a little step forward, then another one back, waiting for Amanda to lose patience and make the first move.

It worked.

As quick as a thought, Amanda lunged, extending her legs, that long arm bringing her weapon shooting in at Della's chest.

Della parried, lunged forward while Amanda was readjusting her stance, and landed a point dead center on Amanda's chest.

"One zero, Della!" shouted their coach Christine, a fit woman in her sixties who had earned a silver medal in the Olympics many years ago.

They readied themselves again. Amanda was too

smart to fall for the same trick twice, so Della wasted no time attacking.

Their swords clashed, the blades rasping against each other. Amanda stopped her thrust, then riposted. Della barely blocked that, and then a flurry of thrusts and parries ensued before Della had the satisfaction of hitting Amanda on the shoulder.

"Two zero, Della!"

It was a hit but not a good one. It came quite close to being a miss.

And now Amanda was getting serious.

She attacked first this time, feinting low and hitting high. Della fell for it, and Amanda landed a spot-on attack.

"Two one Della!"

All Della needed was to get one more hit to win the match. She wanted to win 3-1. She didn't want to just defeat her opponent—she wanted to beat her.

They got into stance. Della jerked a little, trying to get Amanda to react. Her opponent stood as still as a statue. Della jerked a little more, trying to goad her, with the same lack of result.

Fine, have it your way.

She thrust. Amanda reacted just a shade too slowly, caught off guard by her previous two feints.

Not caught off guard enough. Amanda's blade

smacked down hard, leaving Della exposed. Desperately she brought up her blade, turning her body at the same time, Amanda's sword missing her by less than a centimeter.

Della tried to thrust, but she was at an awkward angle, and Amanda had time to parry.

A feint, a thrust, riposte, thrust, and Amanda stepped back, trying to get herself some room so that she could take advantage of her longer reach.

Della didn't let her. She pursued her like a pit bull, launching a whirlwind series of thrusts, feints, and remises until at last Amanda fumbled a parry, and Della's blade made a satisfying impact on Amanda's padded vest, the supple blade bending like a bow.

"Three one, Della. Wow, Della, you're on fire today!"

You don't know the half of it, she thought, as she saluted her opponent and the referee and went to find someone else to beat.

The rest of the hour-and-a-half practice was a series of satisfying wins. By the end, Della was bathed in sweat, her chest heaving, but her mind was at ease.

She and her teammates hit the showers and got dressed. As usual, Della found that fencing had cleared her head, and that the problems of the day that had seemed insurmountable before had now solved themselves in her subconscious.

Now she knew what she needed to do.

First she returned home to drop off her gear, and then, as the long summer twilight began to dim into a gray sky that had finally stopped raining, she returned to the archaeology department.

It was late enough that all the staff had left. If she was in luck, so would have all the faculty and graduate students.

Della used her key to enter the building. She walked through the echoing, empty corridors, her heart in her mouth. She passed one office where a graduate student she didn't know was tapping away on a computer, but he didn't even look up as she went by.

She reached the lab. The door was closed, and no light shone from beneath it.

Looking guiltily over her shoulder, she unlocked the door, flicked on the light, and quickly closed the door behind her.

Everything seemed in place. She moved to the shelves where the finds were stored, found the boxes corresponding to her square, and searched through them.

The brooch wasn't there. Even worse, she could see no documentation either. Even the bag Dr. Olding had put it in was missing.

If the brooch had really been sent down to a lab in London like she claimed, the original bag would contain a slip detailing where the brooch had been sent and why. That was standard procedure, and Dr. Olding always followed standard procedure.

Not this time.

Feeling slightly dizzy, she double-checked. She even checked inside the boxes of the other square she had excavated, thinking it might have mistakenly been put in there.

It hadn't been.

Lucas Lancaster's words came back to her.

Go back to the lab and check on the brooch ... If it's gone, or if it looks like it was made yesterday, give me a ring, and we'll talk further.

Della put everything back in its place and hurried out of the department. She had a call to make.

10

"THANK you for giving me a ring. I was just about to go into town to speak with someone who might know more about this," Lucas said.

"All right. Where shall we meet?" Della asked.

Well, you've certainly come around, Lucas thought. *Things not all well at the laboratory, eh?*

"Let's meet at the bus station. There's plenty of parking there at this hour. He's close by at the Knight Errant."

"The gay pub?"

"Is that a problem?"

Della paused. "No, I'm just ... I didn't think ..."

Lucas laughed. "He is. I'm not."

"Oh."

It was drizzling when Lucas pulled into the bus

station parking lot. Della stood waiting for him under the arcade of a chip shop.

He stopped in front of her.

"So, what happened?" he asked.

"The brooch is gone. She claimed she sent it down to Imperial College London for cleaning. There's no reason why she needed to do that, and there's no documentation saying that she did."

"So, now you believe she stole it?"

Della shook her head, looking grim. "I don't know what to believe."

"Let's go see my friend Richard. He's an expert on all aspects of the occult. He can give us a better idea of what is going on. Come on, the Knight Errant isn't far."

They started to walk, the rain pattering on the hoods of their raincoats.

"Looks like another awkward day in the lab with Dr. Olding tomorrow," Della said. "So, why does your friend want to meet you in a gay pub?"

"It's more that Richard wants to meet you there. He says it acts as a filter. If someone won't meet him at the Knight Errant, they're not worth meeting."

"My cousin is gay. Don't worry, I'm not going to freak out on your friend."

"I'm glad to hear that. And you'll be quite safe.

There are no lesbians there. They all go to the Thistle in Abingdon."

"I've never heard of it," Della admitted.

"Oh right, you have a boyfriend. We've been talking a whole three minutes and you haven't brought him up. I think I've finally convinced you that my intentions are honorable."

"I think your intentions are absolutely crazy," Della muttered under her breath.

The Knight Errant looked like any other British pub except for a rainbow flag hanging above the pub sign, which showed a dashing young knight on a charger with his lance held high. His helmet was off, and his flowing blond hair was far too well styled to be a realistic portrayal of a medieval man. Dance music thudded inside, and as they entered, they saw that half of the interior was taken up by a small raised dance floor. About a dozen men danced alone or in pairs. It was too dark to see clearly, but most looked like university students with a few older men among them.

Lucas led her to the bar area, where they found a few tables, mostly taken. A lone, older black man sat on a stool at the bar, chatting with the bartender. It was Richard, ruling the roost at his usual spot. Richard Camilo worked in some dull administrative job at the university and made up for it by partying well into his sixties at a rate that would kill most people a third his age, and by exploring the deep mysteries of the earth and the civilizations that had lived on it. Lucas knew no one more attuned to the nation's past than Richard.

Lucas waved as they approached, and Richard waved back.

"Della, I'd like you to meet Richard."

Richard turned and smiled at her.

"So, my young friend has finally decided to get a social life. Please don't tell me you have a boyfriend, because Lucas desperately needs to get laid."

Della turned scarlet.

"Steady now, Richard. She's a skeptic. It was hard enough to get her to come here in the first place."

Richard put a hand on his heart and rolled his eyes.

"Oh, I do apologize. I should have worn my Gandalf outfit to convince you I was a wizard. Now where did my long white beard and pointy hat go?"

"Never mind, Richard," Lucas said and laughed. "Gray is definitely not your color."

Richard wore a brilliant scarlet silk shirt and yellow pants.

"A charmer as always. Why, oh why were you born straight? Now what are you girls having?"

"A pint for me," Lucas said.

"Just a Coke, thanks," Della said.

"Not a drinker?" Richard asked.

"Not tonight," Della replied.

"Hmmm, that's quite a long face. Lucas warned me there was trouble brewing."

Their drinks came, and Lucas and Della told him all they knew and had experienced. Della kept stopping any time someone drew near, obviously embarrassed. Lucas tried to tell her that she needn't be, that this was one of the least judgmental places in Oxford, and Richard was well-known for his occult beliefs. Nothing he could do could put her at ease, though.

Once they had finished their story, Richard motioned to the bartender.

"Another pint, please, darling. I need to get the brain juices flowing."

Della sat there impatiently as Richard got his pint, paid, chatted with the bartender about last week's karaoke night, flirted with another customer, and then drank off half his glass. Lucas smiled. Despite appearances, he knew those "brain juices" coursed through Richard's astute mind, trying to put all the pieces together. Of course, none of them had enough pieces to see the whole puzzle, but if anyone could make out a picture, it would be Richard.

"It's a summoning," he said at last.

Lucas swore the temperature in the pub went down several degrees.

"A summoning of ... what?" he asked, his voice shaking a little.

"The entire site is associated with Old Mother Shipton, the best-known witch in the British Isles."

"Oh yeah," Della said. "Someone on our dig was saying there was a legend about her turning a king and his men to stone. You don't seriously believe—"

"No," Richard said. "The story isn't literally true. But Old Mother Shipton traveled far and wide in the 1500s. She became famous for her prophecies and for finding criminals and curing people through magic. It's a wonder she was never tried as a witch. Probably she bewitched the local constables into not hauling her before the court. She's quite a well-known folk figure, and a lot has been written about her. Even more has been written about her in the sort of books Lucas and I read. She was a powerful sorceress, and she almost certainly passed through Oxfordshire. The stories about her turning men to stone out where you're digging are probably garbled memories of some powerful magic she did there. I'm thinking she buried that brooch herself, so that later practitioners who were knowledgeable enough in the ways of the Craft would come and get it."

"Wait," Della cut in. "Are you seriously saying that they're trying to raise the spirit of some lunatic who's been dead for five hundred years?"

"Not quite, darling." Richard motioned for another drink. "They are trying to summon the Earth energy that channels through her. She was a real person, but now she's more of a symbol, an intermediary. Like when the Catholics pray to a saint. They're not really sitting in church praying to some martyr who died centuries ago, they're praying to God through an example of holiness. Old Mother Shipton is only the most recent priestess associated with the Rollright Stones. The stones, as Lucas has probably told you, stand on the intersection of two major ley lines. This nexus point has great power, which is why it has been at the center of worship for so many thousands of years. I think what they're trying to do is to summon up the spirit of that spot, the *genius loci*, in order to twist it to their own ends. The fact that they chased you shows they're up to no good. Plenty of neo-pagans and occultists have done rituals there. I've been out there a number of times myself. We never hunted down intruders, though."

Lucas saw Della shudder at the word "hunted." Yes, that was exactly how it had felt.

"So how does the brooch fit in?" Lucas asked. "It seems more than a coincidence that they were already on the second day of a three-day ritual when Della found it in her square."

"That's a bit of a riddle. For sure it's a synchronicity. It appears Della is linked to all this somehow. Perhaps she has the Gift. I'll wager Professor Olding and her friends hoped the brooch would be found while the excavation was going on. They suspected it was there."

"But they didn't know exactly where because otherwise that would have been the first place for Olding to excavate," Lucas said. He glanced at Della to see how she was taking all this. Her face bore no expression, and she hadn't spoken a word for some time.

"The ritual had to be done on a full Moon," Richard said. "And the full Moon corresponding to a saint's day with a pagan predecessor made it all the more powerful. I think they decided to go ahead with the ritual in any case, hoping they'd find the brooch in the meantime. And that's exactly what happened.

Now their summoning ritual is even stronger. You following all this, girl?"

They turned to Della.

The archaeology student took a deep breath. "I don't believe a word of it. But Professor Olding obviously does. So, the only way we can figure out her next move is to think like she thinks."

Lucas smiled. It was a relief to hear his own words to her echoed back to him. They didn't need her to believe. They only needed her to help.

Richard drained the last of his pint and continued. "The brooch has great power if it's been in the ground that long. Now you said it looked Renaissance. Could it have dated to a bit later? Could it have been sixteenth century, the same time as Old Mother Shipton?"

Della shrugged. "I'm not an expert in Renaissance and Early Modern jewelry styles. Prehistory is more my thing, and I didn't get a look at it after it was cleaned anyway. It could be sixteenth century."

Lucas bit his lip. This was bad. If it was from the time of Old Mother Shipton, it could be associated with all sorts of nasty bits of magic. That was what the Wiccans called the Burning Times, when anyone with alternative beliefs could find themselves at the end of a hangman's noose or even tied to a stake and surrounded by a bonfire. That sort of persecution led to an equal and opposite reaction. There was a lot of vile black magic around in those days, the kind of stuff that made modern-day Satanic rituals look like a tea party at the Methodist Women's Club.

Just what had they stumbled upon here? And how did Della fit into all this? Lucas had been around magic too much to overlook the importance of Della being the one to find the brooch and to forget her phone and have to return to the site at exactly the right time to witness the ritual. Something was working through her, something that wanted to get in the way of this ritual's completion.

He only hoped that something was stronger than what Professor Olding was summoning.

Della brought him out of his thoughts.

"This is all really helpful, I guess, but haven't we lost already? They'll have finished the ritual by now. Haven't they 'summoned' whatever it is they're trying to summon?"

Her tone made it obvious that she thought the danger had passed, that those silly people in their silly robes had done their silly rituals and were now no harm to anybody.

If only.

"It doesn't work like that," Lucas told her.

"Magic isn't like it is in the movies. It's subtle and takes time to develop. What they've done is to start a process, like a chemical reaction. It will take time and probably some more rituals before they get whatever it is they're after."

He turned to Richard for confirmation.

"You've been doing your reading, Lucas. Looks like your aunt has finally gotten you to come around."

Lucas took a drink, not trusting himself to speak. Why the hell did he have to be chosen for the Craft? He hated all of this. Hated that it set him apart from everyone else. Hated that it made him into some sort of guardian for things he couldn't see when all he wanted to do was make furniture and take care of the land.

Most of all, he hated that it had made him an orphan.

"Oh. My. God."

Della's words made him look up. She now sat bolt upright, staring at the dance floor. Lucas turned and looked. He didn't see anything unusual going on over there, just a bunch of guys dancing.

"Has he been here before?" Della asked.

"Who?" Richard asked.

Della pointed. "That guy, the guy in the burgundy sweater and blue jeans."

Lucas saw a man in his early twenties dancing so close to another guy his age that their belt buckles must have been clicking in time to the beat.

"That scrumptious little morsel?" Richard said. "Oh yes, been coming around a lot lately. Why, is he a friend of yours?"

"He's my boyfriend!" Della snapped.

Lucas cringed, then cringed again as Richard did the worst thing he could do under the circumstances —he started shrieking with laughter.

Della got up and stormed onto the dance floor.

11

DELLA COULDN'T BELIEVE her eyes. Her boyfriend was dancing with another man, and really close too.

Now she knew why he had never been very physical with her.

She walked up to him, her anger and hurt overcoming her shyness.

"Hey!" she shouted as she stepped onto the dance floor.

Sebastian turned, and his jaw dropped open.

His dance partner looked at her, looked at Sebastian, looked back at her again, and pointed to the other side of the room.

"I'm going to go that way."

And he did. Quite quickly.

Della turned to Sebastian, her fists on her hips.

"What the hell is going on?" she demanded.

A couple of guys nearby snickered. Sebastian's face turned scarlet.

"I ... um ..."

He bolted out of the pub and into the rain. Della called to him, but he did not look back.

She stood there for a moment, at a loss for what to do.

"Someone just had a rude awakening," one of the guys whispered to his friend. The whisper was loud enough that Della heard. She had the feeling it was intended that way.

Suddenly she started trembling. All these people, judging her! Laughing at her!

She ran to the door, yanked it open, and sprinted into the dark and the rain.

When she finally got home, she buried her face in her pillow and cried and cried until in the early hours of the morning, she cried herself to sleep.

The next morning her alarm woke her. She couldn't face work, not today. She couldn't face the suspicions she had of her professor or even the thought of seeing other people. She texted in that she was sick. Professor Olding, always an early riser, texted back within a few minutes telling her to take care of herself and get better.

In the back of her mind, she knew that might raise some suspicion in her professor's mind, but she had a hard time caring at the moment. All she could think about was Sebastian's betrayal and her own humiliation.

She'd never been cheated on before and certainly not like that.

Wearily she went through the routine of making breakfast. She ate it without tasting the food, then lay on the couch and tried to lose herself in an archaeology journal. Her eyes passed over the words without focusing on them. Her mind kept going back to the night before and all the nights before that.

How could she have been so blind, so stupid? Sebastian was young and healthy, and Della, despite her self-confidence problems, knew she was decent looking. Sebastian had no reason to hold back physically except for the reason that should have been obvious to her. She had refused to see what was in front of her face. Della had told herself Sebastian may have held back because he had some sort of childhood trauma, but he had always talked happily of his childhood. She had clung to that explanation anyway, because she hadn't wanted to face the truth.

So, now what?

"Now nothing," she grumbled as she tried to focus on the journal. "He had no right to lie to you like that. It's over. Damn it, it never really started!"

She tossed the journal across the room. It hit the wall with a smack and ended up on the floor.

So, here she was, single again. She should be used to it by now. High school was a disaster. She didn't have her first love until age nineteen, her first lover at twenty-one. Sebastian was only her third serious boyfriend. He had been handsome, funny, warm, affectionate, and generous with his time. She had gladly overlooked the physical side for all that.

And it turned out all to be one big lie. God, she could kill him!

Her phone buzzed. She whipped it out of her pocket, simultaneously hoping and dreading it was Sebastian.

Instead it was an unknown number.

Della hesitated. The phone continued to buzz.

Finally, she answered.

"Hello, is this Della Marshal?" a man asked. The voice sounded familiar.

"Yes."

"This is Richard from last night. How are you holding up?"

"Um, fine. How did you get this number?"

"Lucas gave it to me. I hope you don't mind. I was wondering if you'd like to talk about your boyfriend."

"Why, so you can laugh at me again?" Della snapped.

"Laugh? I didn't … oh, right. Sorry about that. Had a bit too many. No, really I think we should chat. You must feel awfully confused and upset."

"I appreciate your concern but—"

"If you want to know what's going on with him, I think I can help."

"Do you know him?" She couldn't keep an accusatory tone out of her voice.

"Oh, I never touched the darling lad if that's what you're worried about. But I have seen him around."

"Seen him around?" All sorts of images came into Della's head.

"Why don't we meet somewhere to talk. I might be able to help you understand all this."

Della paused. She didn't want to talk to him. She didn't want to talk to anyone. But he had seemed nice the night before, and here he was reaching out to help.

Stop pushing people away. How many times had

she said that to herself? How many times had she failed to listen to her own advice?

Maybe now was the time to start listening.

"All right," she said, rubbing her temples. She felt a headache coming on.

They met in an old-fashioned café in the covered market a few minutes' walk from campus. Between a gourmet cheese shop and a clothing store catering to tourists sat the narrow, dimly lit little café. The place seemed to have come through a time warp—walls painted a bilious yellow, chipped Formica tables, brown chairs of molded plastic, and black-and-white pictures on the walls of people she assumed were old British movie stars. She didn't recognize a single one.

Richard was already there, dressed in office casual work clothes, a stark contrast to the flamboyant outfit he wore the night before. Still he stood out. He was the only black man in sight. Everyone else was white, mostly older, sipping tea and eating sandwiches or bangers and mash.

Della sat down opposite them, and a middle-aged waitress with a Cockney accent took their orders. Richard asked for a full English breakfast, something people in England ordered at any time of the day. She ordered a tuna fish sandwich.

"How's the food here?" she asked once the waitress had left.

"Terrible. British cuisine is the worst in the world, even worse than American. Only their former colonies saved them from rickets and scurvy. Ever been to a Dominican restaurant?"

"No."

"That's where my grandparents are from. They came over on the *Windrush* in 1948. Became very British. Granddad loved cricket, and my grandmum hung a picture of Queen Elizabeth in the living room. They never gave up Dominican cooking, though. You haven't lived until you've tried *sancocho*. Anyone raised on Dominican cooking can never stomach the fare at somewhere like this."

"If the food's terrible, why did you suggest this place?"

Richard smiled. "You'll see."

"If you tell me the short-order cook is a wizard, I'm leaving."

That earned a look from the pair of little old ladies at the next table. Richard laughed.

"Nice to see you've retained a sense of humor, considering the circumstances."

"I'm trying. It's the only thing that keeps me from going insane."

Richard's face softened. "Not a good night last night, huh?"

"No. It was not."

"I'm sure he feels bad too."

"Oh, I'm supposed to feel sorry for him? He—"

Richard raised a hand. "What he did was wrong. It was unfair, and it was low-class."

When Della didn't reply, he went on.

"I'm not going to defend him, but what he did is all too common. Your cute little graduate student is still in the closet, peeking out to see what he might find. He doesn't know if he wants to come out or not. He thinks having a girlfriend might mean he's straight, and he doesn't have to make a major adjustment to his life and his self-image. But he can't fool himself completely, so he comes to the Knight Errant and dances around."

"He cheated on me."

Richard smiled. "Depends on what you mean by cheat."

"Oh come on!"

They definitely had those two little old ladies' attention now. When she turned to them, they looked away. Della turned back to Richard, too angry to feel embarrassed.

"I've noted that boy coming into the Knight

Errant a few times now. He's quite handsome, and a newcomer is always welcome. I never saw him leave with anyone, and trust me, plenty of people offered."

Della wondered if Richard had offered her "cute little graduate student" a place to go for the night and decided she didn't want to know.

Their food came, so fast that Della knew it had already been prepared and sitting under a heater. For a long time, by the look of it. Her tuna fish sandwich's white bread was soggy and looked as unappetizing as this conversation.

"Even if he didn't sleep with anyone, he's still cheating," Della said.

"Well, if you consider flirting to be cheating, then yes, he's a cheater," he said, digging into some greasy eggs. "I'm not sure I agree, but it's certainly unfair to you. Now your boyfriend, what's his name again?"

"Sebastian." The name tasted like ashes in her mouth. She took a bite of her soggy sandwich to taste something different.

"Sebastian. All right, Sebastian is at a crossroads. He's been fighting these feelings all his life. He doesn't want to be different. He doesn't want the rejection and the labels—"

"This is 2019, not 1979," she said around a mouthful of tuna.

Richard inclined his head. "Oh, you think we've come so far? Sure, our pubs don't get raided by the police anymore. Sure, we can get married. I lived through the seventies, girl, and I remember what hard times were. But the hard times aren't over for some. You know how much homophobia there is in the Afro-Caribbean community? I can't be myself in those neighborhoods. And there's plenty of haters everywhere else too. Plenty of gay bashers, plus the people who smile to your face and snicker behind your back."

"I know all this. My cousin is gay, and his dad absolutely freaked—do you *mind*?"

The last part was directed at the two old ladies, who now openly stared and frowned. Their frowns grew deeper.

"Come on, Ethel," one said to the other. "We've finished our tea, and I sense a foul odor."

The pair got up and walked out, noses in the air.

"You didn't have to be rude," a man in a business suit sitting at another table told her.

"Wait, I was the one being rude?"

Richard waved a hand in front of her face.

"Yoo-hoo! We were talking about your boyfriend."

"My ex-boyfriend," Della corrected.

"My mistake. Ex-boyfriend. Sebastian is trying to find himself, and he probably feels horribly guilty about sneaking behind your back. That's why he didn't go home with anyone. It usually doesn't take long for a new boy to do that after they get the courage to come into the pub in the first place. He tried to stay as loyal to you as he could."

"Look, I appreciate you trying to help, but—"

"But what? You think I'm going to say you should forgive him? Hell no, let him feel guilty, girl! Slap him across the face if it makes you feel better. He deserves it!"

"I'm not really the slapping kind."

"You should try it sometime. Quite invigorating. Look, I'm not trying to tell you what to do about him. I'm just trying to make you understand where he's coming from and to make sure you're not blaming yourself. A lot of wives and girlfriends do when this happens."

Della paused and thought about what he had said. Had she been blaming herself? Perhaps she had a little. She was so awkward socially she tended to assume that when things went wrong in any sort of social situation that it was her fault. In most cases, it probably was. But not this time. Richard was right. This was all on Sebastian.

And the way he described what Sebastian was going through, she felt a little less angry at him than she had before.

She realized she was staring at her nasty sandwich and looked up at Richard.

"Penny for your thoughts," he said.

"Thank you."

She noticed an old couple at another table listening in. The man whispered something to his wife.

"Tell me something," she said to Richard.

"Anything, darling. I am entirely at your service."

"You picked this place just so you could shock people, didn't you?"

Richard let out a loud shrieking laugh that turned the heads of everyone in the place. Della flushed. That sort of campy behavior always struck her as fake and attention seeking, but if Richard wanted to offend a bunch of stodgy old white people, it was certainly the best way.

Della giggled, then choked on some bad tuna fish and ended up coughing it onto the table between their plates. That set them both off, and soon they laughed hysterically. Apologizing in between laughs, they stumbled out of the café and ended up at the nearest pub. It was only noon, and the pub had just opened. That didn't matter. They ordered shots. By one in the afternoon, they were drunk. By two, they were singing show tunes. By three, they had convinced everyone in the pub to play a live-action game of *Ms. Pac-Man*, with Della as *Ms. Pac-Man*, three old drunks as the ghosts, and Richard making remarkably accurate sound effects. By four, Lucas had somehow appeared to drive them home. A good thing too, because Della could barely find her feet, let alone her house.

By sunset, Della lay in her bed with the room spinning around her and her stomach spinning inside her.

"Maybe it's better to be antisocial," she groaned.

12

POOR DELLA, Lucas thought. *What a way to lose a boyfriend. At least Richard showed her a good time. He's good at that.*

Dragging her up to her flat had been a chore, one Lucas had to perform alone since Richard was stretched out in the back seat of Lucas's car with a serious case of the hiccups. Lucas hoped Richard wouldn't get sacked for not showing up at work.

Della had hung on him the entire way up the narrow, steep flight of stairs. A couple of times, she'd slipped, and they almost tumbled all the way back down. That her hair covered half his face and her boozy breath threatened to knock him out didn't exactly help his balance.

He finally found her keys in her purse, opened the door, and deposited her on the sofa.

"You leaving, wizard man?" she had mumbled, trying to focus her eyes.

"Um, yes. Here's a glass of water. You need it."

"Aw, don't leave. Cast a spell on me!" She waved her fingers in the air.

"Must leave. Bye."

"You're cute."

"And you're completely rat arsed."

"Hey! What's wrong with my ass?"

"It's slang for drunk. Night night."

He beat a hasty retreat.

Now it was morning, and he was walking out in the countryside under a light rain. Not the best day for a stroll through nature, especially not for walking, as he was, on top of an exposed ridge. The rain fell from a dark sky that showed signs of getting worse rather than clearing up. At least some trees here and there could help cover him. Sometimes the growth opened up, and he could look to the north across the rolling countryside, the fields and copses like a patchwork quilt.

He was on the Ridgeway Trail, part of an eighty-seven-mile national trail on what was often billed as Britain's oldest road. A clear, straight ridge running along the raised chalk lands of the Berkshire Downs across two counties all the way to the River Thames, it had been a road for five thousand years.

Lucas smiled. The history books were wrong. He knew of older roads, much older. But this road was where he needed to be. The road itself was a ley line, and along its length stood a series of ancient sites. He had already passed a few Neolithic and Bronze Age tumuli, low grass-covered mounds that held the bodies and personal treasures of forgotten chieftains. On the north slope of the ridge a few miles ahead, someone had carved the image of a giant horse at some time in the past. The chalk lay just beneath a layer of turf here, and cutting it away made a figure that could be seen for miles. Along the top of the ridge you could find standing stones, the remains of Roman villas, and the place he was going right now—Wayland's Smithy.

He could feel the pulse of energy beneath his feet as he walked along this powerful ley line. It seemed more powerful, more vibrant, than when he had last walked this path a few months ago. Yes, Dr. Olding and the others were definitely awakening something.

Until now, he had hoped Richard was wrong. He

had hoped the cult was just a bunch of crackpots and not seriously into dark magic.

But he couldn't deny the evidence of his senses. No group of crackpots could have done the ritual this well. Things were awakening in the land, and those with enough knowledge and power could use them to their own ends.

Their own selfish, bad ends.

Dr. Olding certainly had the knowledge. He had seen enough of the ritual to know that. And with that brooch, now she had the power.

And there was that middle-aged fellow, the one with the silvered sideburns. He seemed like he had been in charge. Who was he?

The path continued, broad and straight, with a few trees on either side. To his left it opened up into a field of wheat. He saw the red flash of a fox as it darted into the rows of grain, startled by Lucas's sudden appearance. He smiled.

"Go hide, little fox. If I was a little fox, I'd hide too."

He hadn't seen anyone for an hour. A light rain and the threat of a heavy one weren't enough to deter most English country walkers. That disturbed him. Not that he was alone—because whatever he had to face, he knew he'd be alone for it—but because the normals might be sensing the change in the Earth too. The pulsing energy beneath his feet was not an altogether nice sensation, and unconsciously many people might have decided against walking this path today without knowing why they had made that decision.

That's how magic worked—subtly, often unnoticeably, but far more powerfully than the normals or even most in the Craft understood.

And then, on rare occasions, it would explode into terrible power.

A wave of nausea made him stumble. Before his eyes the path blurred and darkened, and he saw a benighted bedroom—his own—and something reaching from the shadow in the corner.

"Lucas!" his mother shouted, rushing into the room. His father came right behind her.

The thing from the shadow turned on them.

"Stop!" Lucas shouted out loud, and the vision fled.

He stood in the path, the rain hammering down as he gulped for air. Every now and then that night came back to him, the night his parents had disappeared while saving him. Their knowledge of Craft was not enough for what had come out of that shadow in the corner.

His wouldn't be enough either.

He wiped his face, damp from sweat and rain, and forced himself to breathe more slowly. Twenty years had passed since that happened, and then it had been a full moon on All Hallow's Eve. That wasn't a coincidence, and neither was this.

Lucas didn't believe in coincidences. Nobody did who understood the Craft.

Shaken, he pulled out a bottle of water from his day pack, took a slug, and put it back. He squared his shoulders and continued.

Wayland's Smithy was just off and visible from the path. Lucas stopped and studied it before approaching. A low, rectangular mound of grass about two hundred feet long and fifty wide was ringed with stones, some only standing up to his waist, others higher than his head. At the short end of the rectangle, facing the path and the ley line, was the entrance, flanked by a tall pair of stones. Beyond these, a dark hole led inside the mound.

The archaeologists called these monuments Neolithic long barrows, a grave meant for people around 3500 BC. The stones were once topped by a larger mound of earth than in modern times. Back then, only the doorway was visible. The dead would be left exposed until they were only bones and then placed inside. After a time, old bones would be removed and replaced with those of later generations, on and on for years.

The archaeologists were right about everything they said, but they only had half the picture. One of the traits of magic was its local nature, what made up its *genius loci*. If a death ritual were performed over and over again at the same spot for generations, that place would become associated with death magic. It was no coincidence that people saw more ghosts in churchyards and old buildings than in car parks and chip shops.

Wayland's Smithy was an important place for magic of all sorts, especially those that dealt with those who had gone Beyond.

And Wayland's Smithy happened to be on a ley line, a part of the network that crisscrossed the land and included the King Stone, where Dr. Olding's ritual had taken place.

Lucas had a hunch there was a connection, and he had learned to trust his hunches.

He approached, feeling the pulsing from the ley line growing stronger. Places like this served as power points, like relay stations on an electric power grid.

As he reached the entrance, he stopped and

focused. He could feel the different flavor of the power here, the somber taste of death magic. This feeling was not bad. Death was a part of the cycle of life and had to be accepted as such. Every All Hallow's Eve, he would sit vigil through the night next to photos of his parents and grandparents, a candle lighting their way to him. Death rituals were vital to any understanding of a person's place in the universe, but of course some wanted to twist such magic into something foul.

And he sensed something foul now, a taint in the air, not quite a smell but a feeling of unease.

He drew closer. The feeling grew. As he passed between the two entry stones, the feeling became almost physical. He grew aware that the forest had become silent—no birdsong, no breeze rustling the damp leaves, only the regular patter of rain.

The hole into the long barrow consisted of two vertical stones and a lintel, making a stone doorway. Lucas saw a fifty-pence coin jammed between one of the sides and the lintel.

The sight of this familiar folk custom reassured him somewhat. Wayland was an old Germanic blacksmith god with many tales connected to him. The later Germanic peoples had attached their god to this site, imagining it to be his smithy. Even later, after the old gods had faded, there remained a legend that an invisible blacksmith lived here. If you needed your horse shod, you could leave it here overnight along with a coin, and magically the coin would disappear, and your horse would have a new shoe. Even today people left coins as a sort of good-luck offering. Lucas loved that the old ways never entirely faded; they just transformed.

He didn't love that he still felt that foul taint in the ambient magic. That hadn't come from some country walker with a sense of history sticking a coin between two stones.

That came from something that had happened inside.

He set aside his day pack and pulled out an electric torch. Flicking it on, he shone the beam inside to reveal a low corridor. Big slabs of damp stone made up the walls, holding up stone lintels. Here and there, the light shone off coins that people had jammed between the rocks. About two-thirds of the way to the end lay niches to either side, making the entire tomb into a cross shape. Lucas briefly wondered what the early Christians had thought of this.

He crawled forward, pulled by an increasing feeling of dread. His hands grew chilled on the cold, damp earth. The silence increased. He could not even hear the rain now. The still air made the atmosphere inside the barrow heavy and thick.

When he reached the crux of the tomb, where the side niches broke off from the main corridor, his head naturally turned to the left-hand niche.

There he saw them.

A sprinkling of human teeth gleamed sickly in the light of his torch. A portion of skull lay near to it, and worst of all, a human eye lay in the dirt, staring directly at him.

13

DELLA HAD NEVER REALIZED that getting drunk in the afternoon instead of at night meant you would still have a hangover the following morning, but then again, she had never drunk that much before.

She woke up with a mouth that felt like she had spent the night licking the floor of a taxi and a head that felt like that same taxi had run over it.

Luckily Sebastian had taught her a good hangover cure—600 mg of ibuprofen, a large orange juice, and toast covered in thick slices of tomato. Follow this with a long, hot shower and a tall glass of water. Sebastian said it helped a lot.

Oh God, Sebastian.

She tried not to think about his betrayal. The

rain pattered on the window, and she had received a text that it was once again a lab day. She decided to go in. She had a career to build and apparently a mystery to solve, and she wasn't going to let that two-timer stop her from doing either.

Cowardly two-timer as well. He still hadn't sent her a text.

She got herself together and stumbled to the lab, arriving late. Everyone was already there.

Dr. Olding looked up from her computer.

"Della, you made it." Her expression changed when she noticed Della's haggard appearance and pale face, and the big rings under her eyes. "Oh, are you certain you're up for it today?"

"Y-y-yeah, you look t-terrible," Winston said from where he recorded some potsherds into the log.

Della looked at him.

He flushed. "I-I-I mean you look like you f-f-feel terrible."

"I know what you mean, and you're right."

"Must have caught something from that secret boyfriend of hers," Nigel said, glancing over from his drawing of the bone comb he had found and giving Winston a wink.

Winston laughed.

Della grunted and sat down. Dr. Olding came

over and gave her some data to punch into her laptop. A straightforward, mindless task. Just what she needed. Della felt more at ease. Obviously, her professor had no idea that she had been spying on her little cult.

The task turned out to be too mindless, and it gave her too much opportunity to think. Sebastian kept coming up in her mind, as did the conversation she had had with Richard. The older man had put a lot of things into perspective, explaining without defending. She appreciated that. He seemed to have a good head on his shoulders.

So why did he believe in all that occult junk? From what Lucas had told her, Richard was some high priest or wizard or something, going around the countryside performing rituals just like the one she had stumbled on. Lucas probably did the same. It was a case of one set of nutcases opposing another set of nutcases.

Except she couldn't see Richard and Lucas chasing people through the night or stealing historic artifacts.

But she couldn't focus on the mystery of the missing brooch, because every few minutes, like waves hitting the shore, the humiliation of the other night came washing over her. She kept checking her cell phone, hoping and dreading a message from Sebastian. None came. Even though the thought of facing him terrified her, she felt abandoned. She deserved an explanation, and he was the one who should make the first move.

Yes, she would resist the urge to call. He had to do it.

And what if he didn't? What if she never heard from him again?

Della tried to focus—on her work, on what Richard had told them about the ritual, anything except her failed relationship.

The others left her alone, their banter passing over her. She realized that she looked half dead, and the others probably thought she shouldn't have come into work at all.

At lunch time, Dr. Olding got up from her computer and said, "I'm going out. I'll see you in an hour or so. The weather says the rain will clear up this afternoon, and we'll have a string of sunny days. It's back to the field."

The students burst into a chorus of approval. While lab work was interesting, the real fun came from digging things up.

Della tried to imitate their enthusiasm. Normally she would be cheering more than any of them. Right now she couldn't see a positive side to anything.

She left along with the others, breaking off from the crowd to pass through the drizzle to a quiet sandwich shop on a side street where she knew she would be left alone. As she sat alone at a table well away from the windows—she didn't want to run the risk of Sebastian passing by and spotting her—she took out her phone and looked up the phone number for the archaeology department at Imperial College.

She got the secretary and asked to be connected to the archaeometallurgy lab. After a few rings, the phone picked up.

"Imperial College archaeometallurgy laboratory," an older male voice said. "Dr. Tanner speaking."

"Um, hello. I'm from the laboratory at Oxford University, and I was wondering how the work on the brooch is coming along."

"The brooch?"

"Yes, we sent you a brooch, most likely Renaissance or early modern, for cleaning and examination."

"I'm sorry, we've received nothing from you. Are you sure it was sent here?"

"You didn't receive a call from us?" Della asked, her heart beating faster.

"Um, no. There must be some mix-up."

"Oh yes," Della said, trying to sound like she had just realized her mistake. "We sent it to another lab. Sorry for bothering you."

She hung up. For a moment she sat completely still, the world receding from her like a dissipating fog. So, that was that. Dr. Olding really had lied. This was all really happening. Della had been trying to deny it, a little part of her ignoring the evidence and hoping that it was all a big misunderstanding.

No more. She was stuck with the truth. Dr. Olding had stolen the brooch for an occult ritual. Even if the ritual had been harmless superstition, her professor had broken her professional ethics and committed a crime. You could go to jail for robbing an archaeological site.

Now the question was—what to do about it?

She couldn't go to the police. Dr. Olding would just replace the brooch and make some excuse about a paperwork mix-up, and Della would lose her position in the department. Her career would be over before it had really begun.

Even worse, Dr. Olding would figure out that Della had been spying on the ritual. Della would be in danger.

So, it looked like she was stuck trying to do it Lucas's way.

But what could he do? Throw some useless magic at them? That guy was seriously detached from reality.

Although, Della reasoned, so were Dr. Olding and her companions. Sad to say, she knew no one better than Lucas to find out what these people were doing and stop them. If they really were trying some evil ritual, it might end up with them trying to hurt somebody. She couldn't imagine Lucas solving this alone. He was too spacey. She needed to help him build a case against these people. Then she could go to the police and get them busted. If they gathered enough evidence, the police could arrest them before Dr. Olding could ruin Della's career or harm her physically.

She called Lucas and got no response. She tried a few minutes later, and he still didn't pick up. It didn't matter. He'd see that she had called. He'd call back, and they could meet tonight to talk about their next move. It wasn't like she had any plans.

When she returned to the lab, she found Hannah and Evelyn whispering and giggling like a pair of middle-schoolers. Dr. Olding wasn't around, and neither were any of the guys.

"What's up?" Della asked.

"You are not the only one with a secret boyfriend," Evelyn said, making Della squirm.

"What do you mean?"

The French student smiled. "The professor has a handsome man taking her out to lunch today. That is why she is late coming back."

Della shrugged and got back to work. Other people's love lives were none of her business. She couldn't even handle her own. The other two continued to gossip for a while until the others returned one by one from their break. Everyone settled in.

Evelyn was right: Dr. Olding did take a while to return. She usually only took half an hour or so for a quick bite to eat in the faculty lounge. This time she took an hour and a half.

And when she did return, Della nearly fell off her chair.

With her was an older man, a trim fifty-something with graying temples and craggy features.

Della recognized him instantly. He was the man who had led the ritual.

Evelyn and Hannah put on poker faces. The others barely looked up. Della hunched over her work to hide her expression. Out of the corner of her eye, she could see the man looking right at her.

"Everyone, I'd like you to meet someone," Dr. Olding said, her tone uncharacteristically light. "This is Keaton Whitaker of Whitaker Industries. His company made a generous donation that has allowed us to excavate this summer."

That came as a surprise. Della didn't know much about the financial side of the dig, and she had assumed that the university had funded it.

Everyone said hello. Della forced herself to spit out a greeting, tensing as she saw Whitaker still staring at her.

What was that look? Recognition? Suspicion? Or did her own nerves fool her?

Actually, his eager, intent gaze looked more like scientific interest, like how Dr. Olding looked when she held up an unusual artifact to the light to examine it.

Like when she had studied the brooch.

Dr. Olding took Whitaker around the room, introducing each person one by one. To add to the agony, she left Della until last.

"Good to meet you, young lady," Whitaker said in a cultured English accent as he gave her a firm handshake.

"G-good to meet you too," Della replied, trying not to stutter like Winston.

"You sound American," Whitaker said, the smile staying on his face. "We're flattered that you've come all the way here. There are some very interesting ancient societies to keep you occupied on your side of the Atlantic. The Aztecs, for example. A most interesting religion."

Della blinked, trying to figure out if that was a threat. The Aztecs raided their neighbors to capture people to sacrifice to their gods, ripping their hearts out with obsidian knives at the top of their pyramid temples. On high holy days they'd do that to thousands of people. Even the Islamic State hadn't reached that level of bloodthirstiness, although they had given it a good shot.

Della realized it was her turn to speak.

"Oh, um, yes, very interesting. I've always been more interested with Old World cultures, though, especially Europe."

Whitaker's smile broadened. "Good girl. I admire someone who sticks to their roots. Far too many people don't respect their own heritage these days." He turned to Dr. Olding. "Well, Patricia, you certainly have an interesting project. It looks like my money is well invested."

They walked out, chatting away about the excavation as they moved down the hall.

Once Dr. Olding and Whitaker were out of earshot, everyone started gossiping.

"I told you they were dating," Hannah said.

"Patricia? No one calls her Patricia," Nigel said. "For a moment I didn't know who he was speaking to."

"D-did you s-s-see the way she looked at him?" Winston said with a grin.

"*L'amour,*" Evelyn made an exaggerated swoon.

Della put on a false smile. He had stopped to chat with her, and the entire time he had stared at her like some shrink with a new patient. He hadn't chatted with anyone else. Had he recognized her?

Panic almost overwhelmed her. She sat down hard and fumbled with the artifacts she had to catalog. After a minute, she got out her phone and called Lucas. Still no answer. Damn it, where was he when she needed him?

14

"YOU SHOULDN'T HAVE CALLED the police," Aunt Mary said.

"It was a murder, Auntie," Lucas said, huddled in an armchair in the library. "It was a *crime*."

"The boy was right to call them," Uncle Philip said, coming in from the kitchen with two tall glasses of whiskey.

Lucas took his gratefully. His aunt and uncle waited until he had taken a long drink. Then he sat back and stared around at all the books his family had collected over the generations. They provided a lot of answers to a lot of questions, but none could explain humanity's evil.

"What did the police say?" Uncle Philip asked.

"Not much. I told them I was out for a country

walk, went inside to leave a coin for Wayland, and found what I found. They asked me if I had seen anyone, I said no, and they let me go."

"Except your name is associated with the case now," she said.

"Yes, it is," he grumbled. That could be a serious liability.

Aunt Mary shook her head. "It would have been better to have brought those body parts here. There's a ritual we could have done to learn more about how he or she died and another for putting that poor soul to rest."

"It's better to let the police handle it," Uncle Philip said.

"They don't know what's really going on," Aunt Mary countered.

Lucas sighed. That was true enough. The police would try to track down the murderer, but the killers had not likely left any traces. He supposed the police would get DNA off the remains and match them to some missing person, but unless the cult—and he was sure it deserved that hateful label—had been seen abducting that individual, there was little chance of the police solving the case.

No, it was up to him and a nonbeliever who

might have the Talent but was too broken up about her boyfriend to be of much help.

Aunt Mary leaned forward. "So, you say the ley line felt strong, that it pulsed."

"Yes. They have definitely activated something. And those body parts ..." Lucas shuddered again. "That was some foul magic."

"Foul magic rooted in the past. They've brought in Wayland just like they brought in Old Mother Shipton."

Lucas looked up at her. "How?"

"Really, boy, you haven't been keeping up with your reading. Haven't you ever read the *Völun-darkviða*?"

"Read it? I can't even pronounce it."

"Don't joke at a time like this. It's in the *Poetic Edda*. You used to love the Viking sagas as a boy."

"I liked the sagas, not the poetry. I prefer my Norsemen hacking at one another in prose."

"Very funny. The poem includes a version of the life of Wayland, one of the best known versions, and obviously the version these cultists have read."

"And why do you say that?" Lucas asked, taking another long sip of his whiskey. He had a feeling he'd need it.

"In the poem, he's known by his Old Norse

name Völundr instead of the Old English name Wayland. King Niðhad captured him and had him hamstrung. Then he kept Völundr prisoner and forced him to make all sorts of magical items for him. The king had three sons—"

"How unoriginal. Why do kings in these tales always have three sons?"

"Pay attention and stop drinking that whiskey."

"Sorry, Auntie, I'm keeping a fingernail's grip on sanity."

Aunt Mary's face softened. "What you saw was terrible. But if you want to ensure that it doesn't happen to someone else, you had best pay attention."

"Very well then, go on." Lucas set the whiskey glass aside right after taking another sip.

"King Niðhad had three sons, and they were jealous that Völundr, or Wayland as he's known now, was making their father all these fantastic things. They begged him to make them swords and brooches and helmets and all the things young men back then wanted, but Völundr told them that the king had forbidden him from making anything for anyone but him. Then he whispered to each of them individually to come alone and in secret, and in exchange for some gold and mead he would make them whatever they wished. So, each son came in secret, one by one,

one night after the next. When each one showed up, Wayland killed him and made drinking goblets out of their skulls. He made brooches out of their teeth, and his eyes he turned into jewels."

Lucas went pale. "The same body parts I found at Wayland's Smithy."

Aunt Mary nodded, her usually jovial face set with hard lines. "Indeed. And when he made these things, he brought them to King Niðhad as gifts. When the king asked where his sons were, the smith said they were out hunting. Since none of the sons had mentioned to anyone that he was meeting with Wayland at night, no one suspected him. And Wayland laughed as the king drank mead from the goblets of his sons' skulls, and wore the brooch made of his sons' teeth, and adorned his wife with the jewels made of his sons' eyes."

The room fell silent for a couple of minutes. Lucas finished his whiskey, and his uncle refilled it without needing to be asked.

After another sip, Lucas spoke.

"Richard said they were trying to raise the spirit imbued in the myth of Old Mother Shipton. It appears they're trying to do the same with Wayland."

Aunt Mary nodded. After a pause, Lucas struggled to speak.

"I only saw part of a skull and one eye, along with a few teeth. You don't think they actually made a goblet and a brooch and some sort of sick eye jewelry out of that poor man or woman, do you?"

"I wouldn't put it past them," Aunt Mary whispered.

Lucas shuddered and covered his face with his hand. He tried to get a hold of himself, but the trembling only continued. He set his glass down before he dropped it.

"It's happening again, isn't it?" His words came out choked.

"Yes," his aunt said, putting a hand on his. "There's always some foul group that wants to use the Earth's power for evil."

"There's no shortage of evil in this world," his uncle said. "Both in the mundane life and the spiritual life. This time you're big enough to fight it."

"Why me?" Lucas groaned.

"You've been chosen," Aunt Mary said, as she had said many times before. "Perhaps you were chosen even at a young age."

"And that's why Mum and Dad ..."

His aunt and uncle didn't answer. Some things were unknowable.

Lucas sat for a long moment in silence. Then he straightened up and pulled out his mobile phone.

"I need to call Della. She's called me about a thousand times today."

"Go see her," his uncle said. "Impress on her the seriousness of the situation."

Lucas nodded. Uncle Philip did not practice the Craft and avoided it whenever possible, but he knew and respected its power, and his wife had taught him enough to know when the land was in big trouble.

Della picked up on the second ring. She made an appointment to see him at her place. That surprised him. When he suggested a café, she seemed reluctant to go out, and so he agreed.

An hour later, sipping tea in her small living room, a tidy place lined with archaeology and history books, Lucas relayed what he had seen and felt that day. He skipped the part about making jewelry from the body parts. What he told her was bad enough. Della paled.

"We have to tell the police what's going on. They did it for sure!"

"What evidence do we have?" Lucas said. When Della didn't respond, he went on. "We have nothing solid to tell the police, but I know it was them. It fits into the other ritual. They are summoning old arche-types. I presume you are familiar with the phrase?"

"Sure. Symbolic characters that are used in cultures around the world. Everybody in my field has read Jung."

"Exactly. Old Mother Shipton is the crone, the old wise woman. She's also known to some as a witch, either good or bad depending on your opinion. Wayland is the magical smith. Blacksmiths are thought to be magical in all cultures because they can transform one substance into another. Ore into metal. Copper and tin into bronze. Iron and charcoal into steel. Everywhere you look, from ancient Europe to Africa, blacksmiths are said to have magical powers. I know a fellow who has spent quite a bit of time exploring in the Horn of Africa who said that in a certain Ethiopian city the blacksmiths are thought to be werehyenas."

"That's a new one. You have some weird friends."

"You can't even imagine. So, this ritual is a very primal one. They are summoning the spirits of these archetypes. I believe the one we witnessed at the King Stone was only the first. The... remains I found earlier today were quite fresh. I think that poor man or woman was killed yesterday. Goodness knows what the cult's next move will be."

"I have some news of my own. Dr. Olding brought a guest around today to tour the lab. Someone named Keaton Whitaker. Owns a company called Whitaker Industries. He's sponsoring the dig. I recognized him. He was the older guy leading the ritual, the one with the graying hair."

"Keaton Whitaker. Hmm, doesn't ring a bell."

"I figured you'd know all the people into this stuff."

"If by 'into this stuff' you mean practicing wizards, then no. I tend to avoid 'this stuff' like the plague."

"Really? I thought—"

"You thought wrong," Lucas snapped. When he realized what he had done, he continued in a softer tone, "I'm not particularly interested in magic. Unfortunately, I come from a long line of people who have practiced the Craft. That means I have a talent for it, and I'm stuck with it."

"You can give it up," Della said with a shrug.

"It's not like being the agnostic son of the country vicar. You don't choose it. It chooses you."

Della's brow furrowed. "I'm not sure I understand."

"I am quite sure I don't. I'm going to call Richard."

After a quick chat with Richard, who sounded none the worse for wear from the previous day's festivities, they told him what they had learned. Richard said he had heard of Whitaker but wanted to do some more research before giving any advice. Lucas thanked him and rang off. That was one of the things he respected about the old poof—he didn't give an opinion until he actually had something intelligent to say. If only more people were like that.

"He's going to look into it," Lucas said, then noticed Della sat slumped and looking at the floor. "Are you all right?"

Della shook herself as if waking up. "No. Yes. It's just that you talking to Richard reminded me of the other night."

"Oh. I'm sorry."

Della looked at him pleadingly. "What do we do?"

"We? It's your affair."

"No, about Dr. Olding and Keaton Whitaker. To hell with Sebastian."

"Oh, um, right. Look, this has taken a rather nasty turn. It's gone from simply stealing an archaeological artifact to murder. I will not judge you if you back out."

Della shook her head. "No, I'm even more involved than you are." Lucas decided not to correct her on this and let her continue. "You know, when Whitaker met me this afternoon he stared and stared, like he could see right through me. I don't think he recognized me, but he seemed to be interested in me somehow. It gave me the creeps."

He probably senses your talent for the Craft, Lucas thought. *I've been sensing it too. Not that I'm going to tell you. You'd never believe me anyway.*

"So, you'll continue to help?" he asked.

She looked him in the eye. "All the way. But what can we do?"

"It looks like the weather is going to clear up, and you'll be out in the field tomorrow, so I have an idea how you can help. I warn you, though, it's dangerous."

Della's features hardened. "I'm in danger already. Tell me what I can do."

15

THE WEATHER CLEARED up just as the weatherman said it would, which was a bit of a surprise because British weathermen were even less accurate than American weatherman, although correctly predicting anything about the weather in England counted as a minor miracle.

Della made sure she arrived at the dig site first. She squished through the mud in her Wellingtons, glancing to the left and right to check if anyone was watching. The line of trees and underbrush past the King Stone looked dense and threatening, and she remembered how she herself had hidden in them and remained undetected, or at least unrecognized.

She hoped.

As a summer day in England, it was already

light, with the sun winking through the trees and the sky a pale, clear blue. Rich smells of wet earth rose to her nostrils, and the air felt cold and clammy in the June morning.

She moved to where the excavation was covered by a patchwork of tarps, each square outlined by a little puddle of water pushing down the waterproof material. Gingerly she tugged at the end of her square's tarp to slough the water off to the side and onto the grass, then pulled up the tarp fully to reveal her square.

Now came the tricky part. Another glance to check she was alone, and then she shoved the little metal disk into the mud formed by the water that had leached through the edges of the tarp. She smoothed over the mud to hide the hole the disk had made, then moved the mud around a bit to hide that she had smoothed it over.

It still didn't look quite right. A trained eye might notice that the ground had been disturbed, and there were far too many trained eyes on this excavation. Looking over her shoulder to make sure no one else had arrived, she put the tarp back over the square and pushed it down until it pressed against the half of the square where she had put the disk. That way, it would look like she hadn't secured the tarp properly and it had sunk down from the weight of the rain. A simple mistake. Not one she was prone to but believable enough.

Della removed the tarp again and examined her handiwork. It still didn't look one hundred percent right, but it would have to do.

She sighed. Now there wasn't anything to do but wait. She'd putter around the site until everyone arrived, getting rid of the water from the rest of the tarps and greeting everyone like it was just another day. Then Dr. Olding would come and she'd get to work on her square. After a few minutes of work, she'd "discover" the artifact Lucas had given her.

Della shuddered as she went through the motions of preparing the site for another day of work. Her movements were practiced, automatic, the product of a score of months of doing the same thing each morning on digs in the United States, Israel, Ireland, and all over England. But as her body went through the familiar tasks, her mind began spinning out of control.

Winston arrived first, for which she was grateful. If anyone fit in less than her, it was him. She felt a bit cheap thinking that of him, because he was a nice guy, but his speech impediment made him awkward, and thus she never felt anxious around him.

Nigel came next, boastful and flirtatious as always, followed quickly by some of the volunteers.

Della's gut squirmed as Dr. Olding's car appeared in the lane and parked near the King Stone. Her professor strode over to the site, and Della retreated to her square, checking that everything was all right.

Yes, she had smoothed out the mud enough. Not even Dr. Olding had much of a chance of noticing she had seeded the site with an artifact that didn't belong.

Everyone helped unload the tools when Hannah drove up with the van. Dr. Olding called Della over to set up the theodolite, telling her they would expand the site further to the north.

"Thanks. Now how about you get to work on your square," her professor said once they set everything up.

"Sure." Della tensed to hear how that simple word came out in a high-pitched falsetto. She felt like she was broadcasting her fear to the entire crew.

As stiff as some B-movie zombie, she walked over to her square, set out her artifact bags, and started scraping off the earth to be sifted. Angus was at the sift as usual, a safe and kind man, but she didn't dare foist this on him. The disk was too big for her to convincingly miss, which meant she had to call Dr. Olding over and hand it to her herself.

Della hesitated, scraping off the earth with her trowel in the opposite corner from where she knew the disk lay. She worked more slowly than usual, spending time on cleaning each stray potsherd or lithic flake and holding them up to the light.

"Tired?" Angus said as he came for a bucket to sift. His hands were caked with mud from pressing the damp earth through the screen.

"Yeah, didn't sleep well last night," Della said, putting on a plastic smile.

Hurry up and get this over with, she told herself.

Della took a deep breath and started scraping over the spot where she had placed the disk. She worked slowly, methodically, pretending she didn't know what was about to be revealed.

After a couple of minutes, the soft clink of metal on metal told her she had hit it.

Trying to control her trembling, she cleaned around the area as she would with any artifact and revealed what she had hidden—an ornate lead disk with a Latin inscription around a crude depiction of a man with a crocodile head. The disk was pierced at one end so that a cord or a chain could be passed through.

She coughed to clear her throat and called, "Hey, look at this!"

Winston and Evelyn were the closest, and they came over, followed by Dr. Olding.

"W-what's that?" Winston asked.

"I have no idea," Della lied.

Dr. Olding stopped a little away from the square, stared for a moment without being able to hide her shock, and then pushed her way between Winston and Della to crouch beside the artifact.

"Della, Della, Della, you've really outdone yourself this time," the professor whispered.

"What is it?" Evelyn asked.

Dr. Olding paused, as if she didn't want to answer the question but could find no way not to.

"It's Roman. It appears to be a curse. Let me see if I can read the inscription. My Latin is a bit rusty."

She carefully picked up the lead disk and rubbed away the last traces of mud on the surface.

"'Misery to all who defy the wearer,'" she read.

She turned the disk over and continued.

"The sorcerer of Alchester made this."

"C-cool. Alch-ch-Alchester is that Iron Age town near Bicester."

"That's right," Evelyn said. "It's where they found that Roman gravestone a few years ago."

"Yes," Dr. Olding said, still staring at the disk. "There was no Roman settlement at Oxford as far as we know. The nearest was just down the river at Alchester. It was an Iron Age Celtic site the Romans conquered and made their own. Some interesting villas and a cemetery have been found there dating to the Roman period."

"Looks like a wizard was living there too," Della said, trying to make her voice sound normal. "Why is it made of lead?"

Lucas had explained all of this to her, but it was not the sort of information she would have otherwise known, and she wanted to see her professor's reaction.

"Lead was considered a magical metal by the Romans. It was often used in cursing tablets. The curse would be inscribed on the tablet, rolled up, and thrown in a well."

"Sort of the opposite of a wishing well," one of the volunteers said. They had attracted a small crowd now.

"You could say that," Dr. Olding replied. "This was obviously a magical emblem. Note that the figure has a crocodile head. That's probably to represent Sobek, the Egyptian god of the Nile. The Romans were fascinated by Egyptian culture and incorporated many of the gods and goddesses into their belief system. Here, Della, let me bag this for you."

So, you can make it disappear? Della thought as she handed over a plastic bag and a Sharpie. *Good. That's exactly what Lucas and I want you to do.*

Dr. Olding wrote the information on the bag and took the disk away. After a bit more chattering, the crowd broke up, and everyone got back to work. Della released a breath of relief and continued to scrape down the level of soil in her square, finding mundane bits of the past like potsherds and flint flakes. Even coming across a funerary urn from the Bronze Age as she did later in the morning felt like a welcome respite. A dead person was far more comforting than what that disk symbolized.

Della kept an eye on her professor. Dr. Olding moved to the side of the excavation and opened the bag, turning the sorcerer's medallion over in her hands. Then she put it back in the bag and made a call. She talked for several minutes, only stopping when a volunteer approached her to ask her something. The archaeologist got rid of him as quickly as possible and got back to her conversation.

After Dr. Olding hung up, she did a bit of routine work around the site. She had much to occupy her, but Della could see she was excited and distracted, a far cry from the usual cool and collected professional Della had come to know.

During lunch break, Dr. Olding came over to Della where she sat eating a sandwich and sat down beside her in the grass. Della tried to keep her cool.

"I've been quite pleased with your work on the excavation and in the laboratory," her professor said.

"Thank you. I'm grateful for the opportunity."

Dr. Olding lowered her voice. "Don't tell the others, but I think you are the best student I have. The best student I've had in many, many years."

"Thank you," Della replied, wondering where this was going.

"Yes, you have a rare talent. I'd like to discuss your future with you. I think you could go further than you realize."

"Um, okay. I mean, thank you."

"Would you like to have dinner tonight so we can discuss this further?"

Della almost choked on her sandwich. This had not been part of the plan.

"Well, I'm kind of busy but ..." Della realized that an eager graduate student would never say no to this offer. She had to act naturally, and acting naturally meant saying yes. Her next words came out like she was pulling teeth. "I'd be honored. Where shall we meet?"

Dr. Olding smiled. For a second Della thought she looked like a spider that had just caught a juicy bug in its web.

"My house. I'll text you the address, and I'll expect you at seven."

"That would be great," Della said, feeling lightheaded.

When the excavation ended for the day, Della called Lucas and told him what had happened.

"Oh dear. This isn't good."

"You're telling me. What do I do?"

"Go, of course. I don't see a way out of it. If you conveniently fall sick, she'll only invite you another day."

"Ugh, you're right. But what does she want?"

"Tell me your entire conversation, as exactly as you can remember."

Della relayed what she and her professor had said to each other.

"And this was after you uncovered the medallion."

"Yes."

Della heard Lucas let out a long, slow breath. For

a moment there was silence, then some low mumbling as if Lucas were talking to himself.

"All right, Della, it's time you knew. I am sure you won't believe it, but it's important that you hear. I'm a sensitive, Della. That means I can recognize latent magical talent in other people. I sense it in you. It took me a while to notice, because you've buried it under logic and reason, but you actually have quite an affinity for magic."

"Oh, come on."

"You found the brooch, didn't you?"

"So what? That was luck. Someone else on my excavation found a rare Anglo-Saxon coin. Another found an almost perfectly preserved bone comb from the Bronze Age."

"Neither of those are items of magical power."

"And neither is the brooch," Della grumbled. She had been hoping Lucas would give her some good advice. Instead she was getting the intellectual equivalent of a fortune cookie.

"And you forgot your phone on just the right evening and left it at just the right spot in order to witness the ritual. The next day you found the brooch. You are tied to this. Magic happens around you. Dr. Olding senses it too. Whitaker probably does as well. That's why he spoke with you and only you."

"Look," Della said with a frustrated huff. "Just tell me how to handle Dr. Olding tonight."

"Keep your cool. Act like the clueless graduate student who is eager to please her professor. Do not, I repeat, *do not* go anywhere into the countryside with her. Going to her home is perilous enough. If she tries to get you to go somewhere else, get out of there. Make any excuse you can, but beat a hasty retreat."

"Why shouldn't I go into the countryside with her?" Della asked, feeling her blood run cold.

"Because I think she might be trying to recruit you. When she said you're her best student, she didn't mean you're studious. What she means is that you have magical talent. That would be extremely useful to her."

"Recruit me for what?"

"Her organization, of course."

Della shuddered. "She's going to try to get me to join her cult? Wait, what if she wants to sacrifice me like that person you found?"

"She won't do that. She wants you on her side. She can get a sacrifice anywhere."

Della couldn't believe she was having this conversation.

"So why would going to the countryside with her be dangerous?" Della asked.

"Because there are various ways to get you to submit to her will. That brooch has a power similar to hypnosis. When it was glowing in the night, I felt drawn to it. I started to stare at it and not see anything else. My talent and training snapped me out of its hold. You fortunately had enough natural talent for you to snap out of it too."

"I wasn't hypnotized," Della said, feeling uncomfortable. "Okay, I did stare at it, and I did take a couple of steps forward. The whole thing was just so strange that my curiosity took over. That doesn't mean the thing was playing some sort of Jedi mind trick on me."

"Please don't make *Star Wars* references. This is serious."

"I know it's serious. Someone got killed, and I have to go to the home of the killer. You know what I want you to do? I'm going to call you just before I get to the house. Then you're going to call me back two minutes later. That way she's going to see me talking to someone, and I'm going to mention that I'm at her place. She wouldn't dare make me disappear."

"She's not going to hurt you physically, but if it makes you feel better, I'll do it. Just watch out. Don't accept anything from her, no matter how small. If you can't get out of it, ditch whatever it is as soon as you leave. And don't let her draw on you."

"Draw on me?"

"She might try to place magical sigils on you as part of a ritual to get you in her thrall."

"Whatever. Anything else?"

"Be careful."

"Yeah, I figured that. Thanks for your help." Della didn't bother trying to keep the sarcasm out of her voice.

She hung up. What a waste of time.

At least Lucas was right about one thing. Dr. Olding wouldn't risk hurting her in her own house, and Della's plan with the phone call would add some extra insurance. No, her professor really was trying to recruit her. She'd be safe enough at dinner as long as she played along.

So, why couldn't she stop trembling?

16

LUCAS ENTERED the Knight Errant and found it the same as it usually was—thudding music, dancing men, and Richard holding up the bar and chatting with a couple of the other older customers.

"Oh look, it's Harry Potter," one of the men said.

Lucas smiled at the old joke. Jake was a brick-layer from Abingdon, a portly working-class man who broke pretty much every societal stereotype about gay men. He even liked football.

"Hello, lads," Lucas said. "I need to speak with Richard alone if you don't mind."

Something in his tone kept them from making the predictable reactions. They nodded, Jake clapped him on the shoulder, and they moved off.

"This sounds serious. Let's move to a table," Richard said.

Lucas glanced around the dim interior. "None are available."

"I'll take care of that, darling." Richard moved over to a table where two young men were talking. "Girls, next round's on me if you shove off and give us this table."

The men glanced at each other, shrugged, and headed to the bar.

"Students," Richard said with a grin. "Such whores for a free pint."

As Lucas sat down, he glanced at the dance floor.

"Oh, he's not come back," Richard said. "His dramatic exit certainly got the girls buzzing. Do you think you could get him and your new girlfriend back here for some more drama? It's terribly amusing."

"She's not my girlfriend, and thanks for talking with her. I think it helped."

"Getting her lashed on a noontime pub crawl helped. Now how can I help you?"

Lucas grew serious. Leaning forward, he told Richard about everything that had occurred since they last met. Richard's face went grim, taking on hard features like those of an ancient sculpture.

Once Lucas finished, Richard sat and thought for a moment.

"That poor fellow. Why do people have to twist the Craft this way? Your aunt is correct. They are touching on the *genius loci* of various sites, channeling them through archetypical figures associated with them. It's Earth Magic but Earth Magic tied to folklore."

"Why?"

"I did some research on Keaton Whitaker. He's the owner and CEO of Whitaker Industries, an engineering firm that has numerous contracts with the Department of Defense, all classified. What's more interesting is that he has funded numerous archaeological excavations all over the world and is known in the collecting world for making major purchases of antiquities."

"Legitimately?" Lucas asked. The antiquities trade was notorious for selling stolen items, especially from war zones where things could be smuggled out of the country easily. Quite a lot of Mesopotamian artifacts had disappeared from Iraqi and Syrian museums in recent years. Some of them got traced and returned to their countries of origin, but the vast majority disappeared into private hands.

"As far as I can tell, yes. He specializes in religious items—statuettes, inscriptions, that sort of thing. He bought a Roman marble altar to Mars last year."

Lucas whistled. "That must have sold for a pretty penny. But you haven't told me why they are doing this type of ritual."

"I'm getting to that. You wouldn't be so impatient if you had been initiated properly."

"I don't want to be initiated. I don't even want to be a part of all this."

Richard inclined his head. "You and I both know that we don't get to choose. I've done a bit of asking around about Whitaker and confirmed some things I suspected about him. He's into the Northern traditions, and not in a good way."

Lucas didn't have to ask. Each region had its own pagan traditions, rooted in the pre-Christian past. While nothing was wrong with that in and of itself, some practitioners twisted that localism into xenophobia. A couple of years ago, Lucas went to a Druidic ritual at Stonehenge with Richard, and a couple of toughs told him to go back where he came from. When Richard blithely asked when the next train to London was, they escalated to name-calling.

Luckily the Chief Druid intervened and threw the racists out, then apologized profusely to Richard.

People like that weren't welcome in respectable magical orders, but there were plenty around.

"Is he in one of the neo-Nazi magical orders?" Lucas asked.

"None that I know of. He seemed to be into his own thing. I've heard whispers that he funds some of the banned nationalist political parties as well, but I can't get confirmation. As you can imagine, I don't have many contacts with that sort. But here's the motivation—Whitaker's son was in the British army. He got killed a couple of years ago by an ISIS road-side bomb in Iraq."

Suddenly everything was clear. This was some sort of magic intended to hurt outsiders. Whitaker, Olding, and the rest were summoning the spirit of the land to eject what they saw as a foreign invasion. Just how that would manifest, he wasn't certain, but it was sure to be bloody.

"Of course," Lucas whispered. "Everyone at the ritual was white. Why didn't I notice that before?"

Richard smiled. "Because white is your default setting. You assume people will be white unless you go somewhere you usually don't go."

"Oh, come on. Most practitioners are white. It's because—"

"Most practitioners aren't white, it's just that

you don't get invited to the black rituals. Or the Asian or Arab rituals. But you get to go to one now."

"What do you mean?"

"We're going up to Wayland's Smithy. Right now. We have a spirit to lay to rest."

Lucas hesitated. "Won't that be dangerous?"

"Of course it's going to be dangerous. And if I'm right about the kind of magic they're casting, it will be far more dangerous for me than for you."

They got into Lucas's car and swung by Richard's house, a little one-bedroom place at the far end of Cowley Road opposite a Halal butchers and a Jamaican restaurant. Most of the people on the street were East Asian or Middle Eastern. Though he was born in London, Richard preferred living in the immigrant neighborhood. Richard had told him several times how the superficially liberal whites of Oxford used many subtle ways to make it clear he wasn't welcome.

Lucas paced in Richard's living room while the magician rummaged around the house, gathering various materials.

"Which ritual is this?" Lucas asked as Richard loaded him down with a duffle bag and seven heavy and very old-looking iron candlesticks.

"Typical spirit-laying ritual, with my own twist. I'll walk you through it."

"The power up there felt strong."

"And it will get stronger with every passing night. Plus, they have other rituals planned, I'm sure of it."

"I know. We're laying a trap for them. I had Della pretend to uncover that sorcerer's medallion of my aunt's. You know, the one that mentions Alchester?"

Richard's jaw dropped. "Are you insane? You just handed over a magical item to those bastards."

Lucas smiled. "I'm one step ahead of you, my friend. I do a bit of metalworking in my workshop. Sometimes I need to mold furniture fittings. Well, I created an exact replica."

"And your darling auntie cast a glamor on it so they can't tell a fake from the real thing," Richard said with a grin. "So, is the plan to trick them into doing a ritual at Alchester with you throwing a spanner in the works?"

"Me and Aunt Mary. She's better at this sort of thing."

"You're coming along, Lucas. There's hope for you yet. What does your girlfriend think of all this?"

"She's not my girlfriend, and she's on board. I

told her about the murder, and she understands how serious this is."

"No, she doesn't," Richard said, ushering him out the door and back to the car. "She's an unbeliever."

"Dr. Olding is working on that."

"What do you mean?"

"She invited Della over to dinner. Probably to recruit her."

"And you let her go? Are you quite mad?"

"They're not going to hurt her. She's got the Talent. I'm sure you sensed it quicker than I did. They're going to try to win her over."

Richard let out a long breath of air through his clenched teeth as Lucas started up the motor. "It's still a hell of a risk, though."

"We're all taking risks. And she's too involved in this already to stand on the sidelines. I don't like it either, but she's safer as a participant than as some clueless bystander."

"At least the boyfriend is out of the way. Don't need him blundering through all this."

"I think he's blundered enough," Lucas said.

There was no way to drive to Wayland's Smithy, so Lucas had to park on an isolated country road, and they huffed it up the ridge, hopping over fences and squishing through damp fields. Richard cursed as the mud ruined his shoes and soaked his socks. Lucas, as usual, wore his work boots. The sky was mostly clear, with a few moonlit clouds scudding overhead. Their way was well illuminated by the Moon, only a couple of days past full, and even when it went behind a cloud, the Moon left light enough for them to see the ridge looming ahead.

By the time they reached the top of the ridge, Richard was huffing and out of breath.

"Maybe you should join a gym," Lucas said.

"Maybe I shouldn't get mixed up in stuff like this," Richard replied, leaning against a tree as he tried to catch his breath.

"If this ritual is what I think it is, it'll come at you eventually."

"Me and everyone else on Cowley Road. Let's go."

They walked through a patch of forest and a field of grain before making it to the path.

"Whoa," Richard said as they stepped onto the ley line and felt its recently awakened power.

They walked the half mile to Wayland's Smithy in silence. When they got there, they saw a police notice affixed to a tree. Richard shone an electric torch on it and saw it announced that the site was closed as a crime scene and no one could enter under penalty of law. They passed this sign, ducked under some police tape strung between two trees, and strode to the barrow.

Here they paused, not because of the police tape crisscrossing the entrance, but because of a wave of nausea that hit them both in the gut. The feeling emanated from the barrow like a foul odor. Every instinct screamed at them to turn tail and run.

They stayed there, although they did take a few steps back.

Richard turned off the torch.

"Do you have to do that?" Lucas asked.

"Do you want to be spotted?"

"Wouldn't mind the company."

Richard took the duffel bag from Lucas and pulled out a smudge stick of herbs. Igniting it with a lighter, he passed the smoking stick over Lucas, who felt a tingling all through his body. The nausea eased a little, but the fear remained. Richard then smudged himself, stepped forward and made several passes over the entrance, and then circled the entire barrow. Lucas felt a spike of panic as Richard passed behind the barrow and out of sight. When he returned to where Lucas stood, he extinguished the smudge stick.

"Ready?" Richard asked.

"No."

"Neither am I."

They went to the entrance and tore the police tape away. The heavy scent of sage and other herbs hung in the air, a slight reassurance as they faced the darkness inside, like clutching a life preserver as a tsunami hit your ship.

They didn't get a step past the threshold before the tsunami hit them.

A wave of cold malevolence and nausea swept over Lucas, who staggered back shivering. Richard, the more experienced occultist, held his ground, whispering an incantation under his breath. Pulling a candle out of the duffel bag, he stuck it in one of the ancient candlestick holders and lit it.

The light the little flame cast seemed unusually feeble in the enclosed space and did not reach the back of the chamber. The shadows there seemed almost solid. Lucas couldn't even see the entrance to the side chambers.

But a little light was better than none, and as Richard continued chanting a warding incantation, Lucas regained his strength and joined him in lighting the rest of the seven candles. These they set with trembling hands in a line from the entrance into the interior of the barrow. The shadows seemed to withdraw reluctantly, fighting the light. The ceiling was so low that Lucas and Richard had to squat as they moved, and the confined space felt stuffy and oppressive.

The fifth candle they placed at the intersection of the main passage and the side niches, the last two at the back of the barrow. While they did this, they didn't dare look into the niche where Lucas had found the body parts. Not until the line of enchanted candles was finished, a spiritual lifeline out of this cursed place and back into the natural world, could they summon the courage to look inside.

They saw nothing but felt all too much.

A sense of dread wafted out of the niche like a cold wind. Lucas shuddered. Both men sat down, all but overcome by the evil emanating from that space. Richard seemed to move in slow motion as he unloaded various magical tools for the laying of the murder victim and the exorcism of the darkness that the killing had summoned.

Richard set down a crystal bowl and filled it with pure oil. He set a wick of twisted herbs in the bowl and then lit the wick. Next, he pulled out a little brass bell and rang it three times. The pure, sharp note sounded strange in such a dank, muffled interior space. Throughout all this, Richard continued his low chanting in a language Lucas did not under-stand. It sounded like some ancient Caribbean native tongue, probably a language that everyone assumed was long dead. But just like the English, the islanders kept their own traditions and passed on their own secrets.

Lucas did not know this ritual, so he helped the only way he could—by focusing intently on the light and the sounds of the spell and picturing the spirit of that poor man or woman going to a place of peace and rest. This focusing was a form of meditation, a type of mental practice in which an onlooker could increase the power of a ritual. Members of more stan-dard congregations did it all the time without being entirely aware they were doing it.

As Richard continued his chanting, he pulled out a vial of water that he poured into another crystal bowl. He dipped a brush of fine hairs into the water and flicked the drops onto the niche's sides, floor, and ceiling.

Lucas felt the atmosphere subtly change. The space felt less enclosed. The slabs of stone that made up the roof, although only a couple of feet above their heads from where they sat, seemed to lift. The air smelled cleaner. The shadows receded as the candles grew in brightness.

It's working, Lucas realized. *Who would have thought a Caribbean ritual would work in an English long barrow? I guess spirits are the same everywhere.*

Lucas set those thoughts aside. The best thing he could do for the poor murdered soul was focus on putting it to rest. He set about this with a renewed act of will, pushing his vision of peace and tranquility into the space before him. The candle flame waxed, and a fresh breeze seemed to whisper through the barrow.

Richard sensed the change too, and his chanting became louder, more confident. Again he rang the little bell three times, its pure sound resonating off the old stone walls and lintels.

A clang of metal on stone from the direction of the barrow entrance sent an iron bar of tension up Lucas's spine. He didn't even jump at the sudden, unexpected sound. He only froze. All at once, the air became oppressive again, and the walls seemed to close in, the roof lowering.

The light dimmed too as a shadowy veil like a funeral gauze permeated the air.

Glancing toward the entrance, Lucas saw the candle by the entrance snuff out. Beyond lay only blackness.

Another clang reverberated through the barrow.

Lucas felt it in his gut like a distant explosion. Something snuffed out the next candle.

"Richard... what is..."

He realized Richard wasn't chanting anymore. He turned to his friend and saw him pressed up against the wall, eyes bugged out, his mouth working but no sound coming out.

Clang. The third candle was snuffed out. The clanging was loud, like a hammer hitting the stone wall of the barrow.

Like a hammer, Lucas thought.

A smith's hammer.

Oh no.

Lucas started chanting an Old English ward against evil his aunt had taught him. He didn't know the accompanying ritual, or if indeed any existed. He wasn't even sure he was pronouncing all the words properly, but it was the only protection he had.

Clang. The next candle was snuffed out. The darkness drew closer. He could almost reach out and touch it now. Waves of malevolence washed over him, but Lucas realized that they were not directed at him personally. No, they were passing him by and aiming at Richard. That was why he was paralyzed even though he was the more accomplished wizard.

A spell against outsiders. Richard was right. Wayland is targeting him because he's not European.

Lucas shifted a little so that he crouched in between Richard and the approaching darkness. He continued his Old English spell, chanting it more loudly, coming to the end and beginning it again. The fifth candle, the one at the intersection of the main passage and side niches, sat just inches from his feet.

Clang. The noise was deafening, and Lucas swore he felt the whoosh of air as something large passed inches from his head before hitting the wall and making that ear-splitting noise.

Still chanting, Lucas grabbed the bowl of blessed water that Richard had been using in the ritual and splashed it at the darkness. The water disappeared into that black wall with a hiss.

Lucas grabbed the bell, ready to ring it, hoping its pure sound could somehow counteract that horrible, unseen hammer.

He never got a chance to try. All at once, the other two candles were snuffed out at the same time and he felt a powerful force lift him up and dash him against the wall.

Just before he lost consciousness, he heard Richard scream.

17

DELLA ARRIVED at seven o'clock on the dot, with a fine bottle of French white wine tucked under her arm. She knew a lot about expensive wines thanks to Sebastian. At least she had gained something from that failed relationship. The bastard still hadn't called her.

Good riddance.

Instead she had to rely on a self-declared wizard who thought magic was real.

At least Lucas called her, right on schedule just as Dr. Olding opened the door, the smell of a roast wafting out into the evening air.

Della smiled apologetically at her professor as her phone started to ring. She handed Dr. Olding the bottle, got her phone out of her purse, and answered it.

"Oh, hi, Bill. Sorry, I'm a bit busy right now. I'm going to dinner at my professor's house. Yeah, Dr. Olding. I told you about her. I'll call you when I leave. Bye."

Dr. Olding didn't bat an eyelid. That made Della feel a bit better. Only a bit.

"Sorry," Della said as she hung up. "Someone I'm meeting up with later tonight."

"Not a problem. Come on in."

Della crossed the threshold. She had never been in Dr. Olding's house before, and as far as she knew, neither had any of the other students. Under normal circumstances, she would have felt honored. Now she only felt terrified.

Passing through a front hall adorned with old prints of various university buildings in Oxford, they entered a living room. It was larger and better furnished than her own but similar in that it was mostly taken up with books.

"Make yourself at home," Dr. Olding said. "I'll put this in the refrigerator. Would you like anything? I have a bottle of red already open."

"That would be lovely, thanks." Then, remembering something Sebastian had told her, she added,

"It's too bad I didn't know you were cooking a roast, otherwise I would have brought red instead of white."

"That's all right. We can have it after dessert."

Dr. Olding left. Della took the opportunity to examine the nearest bookshelf.

The volumes were all what she expected— archaeological books and monographs, plus some rare early issues of the leading journals.

She moved to another shelf and found it filled with old volumes, their leather bindings and anti- quated fonts suggesting the nineteenth and eigh- teenth centuries. Some were on archaeology, but the majority were on English folklore or anthropological studies from around the world. She saw a great deal on world religions.

Nothing on magic, though. No grimoires on occult practices or demon summoning, not even any New Age stuff on meditation or astral projection. Della supposed that sort of thing would be hidden away.

Some of these books hinted at Dr. Olding's real interests, however. Della pulled a volume off the shelf titled *Religious Rituals of Central Africa*. The title page gave a London publisher and a date of 1806. The table of contents showed that while some of the chapters focused on African cosmology and the various gods and goddesses, the bulk of them concerned the spirit world, magic, and interviews with witch doctors.

"Interesting library, isn't it?" said a man from behind her.

Della gave out a little yelp and whirled around.

Keaton Whitaker stood in the doorway, two wine glasses in his hands.

"Oh dear, I seem to have startled you. Don't worry, I'm not the boogeyman."

"Sorry," Della said, her heart threatening to rip out of her chest. "You just gave me a fright."

"I can see that. I do apologize." Whitaker held out both glasses. "A Spanish Rioja or an Italian Sangiovese?"

"I, um, the Rioja, thank you." Della took it.

"A good choice to go with the roast. You know your wines."

Della was too confused by his sudden appearance to come up with a response.

At least I know the wine isn't spiked since he gave me a choice, she thought. *Oh my God, why didn't I think of that risk before I came here? You're standing in front of a murderer!*

Calm down. They're not going to kill you. They want to recruit you, like Lucas said.

And if I say no? What will they do then?

While she thought this, Whitaker talked about the dig and how interested he was to see its progress. Della nodded politely, not really taking in his words.

Dr. Olding appeared behind him with her own glass of wine.

"Oh, I forgot to mention that Keaton will be joining us tonight. I hope you don't mind."

"Oh, delighted," Della replied, her voice a frightened warble.

"And what do you have there?" Whitaker asked, taking the book from her hand. "Ah! African religion. Interesting topic. I think the animists are closer to the truth than the monotheists, don't you? The idea that every living thing, and even unliving things, is resonant with its own energy, is a most compelling theology. And one backed up by quantum physics."

"I never gave it much thought," Della said, unsure where this was going.

"Ah, that is because you are young. The young never think much about religion or the meaning of life."

"I had a roommate in my dorm in sophomore

year who was in Campus Crusade for Christ," Della said.

A cloud seemed to pass over Whitaker's face.

"The holy rollers think about it even less. I hope the silly girl didn't convert you."

Della was trying to figure out a reply when her professor saved her.

"We're not here to talk about religion, Keaton," she said with a laugh that Della did not find convincing. "We're here to talk about Della's career."

"Ah yes, forgive me," Whitaker made a little bow. "Patricia has told me good things about you. You have an obvious talent."

Della remembered what Lucas had said to her. Of course these people weren't "sensing" any magical power in her, because there was none to sense, but if something so simple as finding the brooch could catch their interest, Whitaker's words could have a double meaning.

"I certainly seem to be lucky on this dig," she said.

Whitaker took a sip of his wine and smiled. "There is no such thing as luck."

"Well, scientifically speaking, random chance doesn't pick favorites," Della said. "But sometimes it moves in someone's favor."

"Ah yes," Whitaker said softly. "Science."

Unsettled, Della turned to Dr. Olding. It was time to do some fishing.

"I'm so excited about that Roman sorcerer's medallion. I've never found anything like it. So, when are you going to tell the press? A find like that will make national news."

Dr. Olding's reaction was the same as Lucas had told her it would be.

The professor's mouth tightened into a firm line, and she said, "We won't be telling the press until the time is right."

The way Dr. Olding said it, Della sensed the time would never be right.

"But it could help with support for the dig," Della objected.

"The excavation will have all the support it needs," Whitaker said. "I'll make sure of that."

"I'm just thinking the public would be interested. It's the sort of find that helps archaeology remain popular," Della said.

Dr. Olding smiled. "Don't worry. We'll have a big press release once we're ready. But let's talk about you."

She sat on the sofa, and Della took this as a sign that she should sit too. She picked an armchair a little bit away from Dr. Olding. Whitaker sat right by her professor on the sofa, rather too close for a professional relationship. Della realized the laboratory rumor machine had guessed right.

"Yes," Whitaker said, studying her again. "We think you are quite promising. You might not know this, but I sponsor a number of excavations across Europe. I have one I'll be starting next year in France. Are you familiar with the Battle of Tours?"

"That's when the Franks stopped the Muslim invasion from Spain."

Whitaker's eyes lit up. "Exactly. The Umayyads had taken most of the Iberian Peninsula and in the year 732 tried to enter France. Charles Martel stopped them in their tracks. He saved France and perhaps all of Europe. The victory also helped found the Carolingian Empire, one of the high points of the early Middle Ages. It was the beginning of Europe's renewal."

"It certainly sounds like an interesting project. I've never done any medieval archaeology. But I thought the site of the battlefield was lost."

"We'll start with a survey," Dr. Olding said, edging closer to Whitaker. "The battlefield is known to be somewhere near the hamlet of Moussais-la-Bataille in France. Oral tradition and the name itself all point to the location being close. We think you'll be perfect for the project."

"I'm flattered," Della said.

"This will be a paid position," Whitaker said. "Generously paid."

"That's most kind of you. Wouldn't you rather have a medieval expert?" Della couldn't recall Dr. Olding ever mentioning excavating any sites from the period or any sites in France. Like Della, her professor specialized in British prehistory.

"We'll have some," Dr. Olding said. "But we think your unique talents will be a great help."

"My unique talents?" Della asked. Lucas's words came back to her. Yes, they really did think she was some sort of magical person.

What idiots, she thought.

Dangerous idiots. You need to be careful.

Whitaker leaned forward, his eyes afire.

"You have a sense of the land, Della. That brooch, that medallion. You have a natural talent for finding important things that are hidden. And think of how important this battle was. If not for Charles Martel and his brave knights, Europe would be Muslim. You'd be wearing a veil and be hidden away inside your husband's house. There would be no great art, no science, no creativity."

"The Muslims made a lot of art and science," Della objected. "During the Middle Ages, they were more advanced than Europe."

"Bah!" Whitaker swept his hand in a dismissive gesture, almost smacking Dr. Olding in the face. "Modern politically correct nonsense. A rewriting of history to assuage the immigrants. Most of the so-called 'learning' in the Islamic world was stolen from the ancient Greeks or done for the Arabs by the Jews or Coptic Christians. We hear so much about Muslim tolerance in the Umayyad and Abbasid empires, but that was because they needed the subject peoples to make all their great accomplishments. Did you know that for centuries the cloth that was put over the Kaaba in Mecca was woven by Coptic Christians? They were the best weavers in the so-called Muslim world. Do you know who built the great architecture of Isfahan? Armenian Christian architects. Who sculpted the gorgeous stonework of the Taj Mahal? Hindu craftsmen. The Muslims have not produced a single thing of—"

"Keaton," Dr. Olding chided.

Whitaker smiled at her, then turned back to Della.

Is this a millionaire wizard or a spokesman for the English Defence League? Della wondered.

"Forgive me. I sometimes get carried away. It's just that our culture is under attack from without and within. If we aren't careful, Western civilization will go the way of the dinosaurs."

Okay, so he's both.

Della said, "I don't think Western civilization is going to disappear. It's just undergoing some changes."

Whitaker frowned. "Changes for the worse. We've lost our sense of place, our sense of self. Listen, Della, I know you know what I mean. You love the past. You crossed an ocean to excavate in the land of your ancestors. And how many times did you have to hear from people your age, 'Oh, why do you want to study that stuff? Who cares what happened a thousand years ago?'"

"A lot," Della conceded.

"Exactly. People don't care about their past, about where they come from. And if they lose that sense of identity, what are they left with? This is why we're going to search for the battlefield of Tours. Why does one of the most important events in European history, one that shaped the course of our civilization, not have a museum? Not even a historical marker on the correct spot? Why hasn't the government of France, or the European Union, allocated funds to search for it? I'm honored to perform the service, but why do I even have to?"

"Well, it's most generous of you ..."

Whitaker's eyes lit up. "This will be the find of a century, and you can be right there when it happens. I want you to be part of it."

These people are absolutely crazy, Della thought. *Just look at Whitaker's face. He looks like some cheap televangelist. And Dr. Olding is just sitting there all meek and mild.*

As if on cue, her professor looked at her watch and said, "The roast should be ready. How about we eat?"

Good Lord, she's acting like a housewife with this guy.

They got up and went to the dining room. Della followed.

There, they really started putting pressure on her.

18

LUCAS AWOKE to a splitting headache and a blinding light in one eye. The harsh rasp of a radio chattered nearby, then cut off sharp. The light went out. Someone opened his other eye, and the light came back.

"He's coming to," he heard a female voice say. "Sir, can you tell me your name?"

"Richard?"

"All right, Richard, you've had—"

"No, Richard is my friend. Is he all right?" Lucas tried to sit up, but his movements were weak and clumsy. A gentle but firm hand pressed him back down onto the padded surface on which he lay.

"Your friend is going to be all right," the female voice said again.

The bright light moved away, and Lucas blinked, looking around him. He lay on a stretcher in the back of an ambulance. A South Asian woman in an emergency worker's uniform knelt beside him. Looking down past his feet, he could see the night outside. A second ambulance was parked nearby, as was a police car. They looked like they were parked on a country road.

"What happened?" he asked.

"That's what I want to ask you," a police officer said, appearing at the opening of the ambulance. The officer, a gruff older man with a graying crew cut, turned to the emergency worker. "Is he all right to be questioned?"

The woman nodded. The policeman turned back to Lucas and motioned him to come out of the ambulance.

Lucas sat up. He ached all over, and his head throbbed. When he brought his hand to it, he found it was wrapped in gauze.

"Just a bad bump," the emergency worker said. "There's no sign of concussion. You'll be all right. So will your friend."

Gingerly, Lucas got out of the ambulance.

As soon as he did, the cop turned him around and cuffed him.

"I am arresting you for trespassing on a crime scene. You and your friend will need to come down to the station. What's your name and current address?"

Lucas told him.

"Is there anything in your pockets I should know about?"

"No."

"No needles? Drugs?"

"No!"

The officer searched him, checking the ID he found in his wallet.

"Can I see my friend now?" Lucas asked.

"You'll see him down at the station. Now how about you tell me what you were doing up there?"

Lucas took a deep breath. The truth, or at least as much as this fellow would believe of it, seemed the best course.

"I was the man who reported finding the body parts in Wayland's Smithy. My friend and I are pagans. We think the victim was sacrificed in a black magic ritual. Since this is a spiritual site, we decided to lay the spirit of the victim to rest and try to banish the evil spirit the murderers were trying to raise. When we were in there, something—I mean someone—blew out the candles and attacked us."

To the policeman's credit, he did not look fazed by this unorthodox explanation.

"So, you ignored the warning signs, tore away the police tape, and trampled all over a crime scene."

"Um ... well, if you put it that way, it looks rather bad."

"Indeed it does. To put your mind at rest, no boogeyman attacked you. I and my partner saw your parked car and were able to track you up the side of the ridge and to Wayland's Smithy. We've been keeping an eye on this area since the murder. We were approaching the entrance and saw your candles and heard your chanting. Just then, a wind blew right into the entrance and blew out all your candles. The two of you must have panicked, because I heard you both screaming bloody murder. When we got there and shone our torches on you, you had both knocked yourselves out. Probably jumped up and bashed your silly heads against the roof. You're lucky you didn't get more seriously hurt."

That's not what happened, Lucas thought. *That's what you saw with your mundane eyes. On the spiritual plane, we came close to being murdered.*

"Sounds like you came just in time, Officer," he said. That was true enough. The spirit of Wayland had been targeting them outside the normal plane of existence, and the intrusion of the two police officers had broken the spell. He dreaded to think what would have happened if either of the police officers hadn't been English. The woman in the back of the ambulance was of Indian descent. Good thing she got called in later.

Within a few minutes, he was sitting in the back of a patrol car with Richard, heading to the Oxford city police station. They said little. Richard seemed a bit dazed and had a large bandage on his temple but otherwise looked unhurt.

At the station they were processed, questioned again, and then left in the interrogation room twiddling their thumbs for half an hour. Finally, the detective who Lucas had spoken to when he reported the body parts showed up. A trim man in his late thirties, he entered the interrogation room, studied the pair for a moment, and sat down across the table from them.

"I'm Detective Chief Inspector Matthews. Mr. Lancaster, you and I have already met. Mr. Camilo ... or do you prefer *Señor*?"

"Mister is fine. I was born and raised in London. I've met white people who speak better Spanish than I do."

"All right. Mr. Camilo. It appears this isn't your

first charge of criminal trespass." DCI Matthews looked at a small notebook. "In 2009, you were arrested after dark at West Kennet Long Barrow. In 2011, you and five others were arrested after dark at Mons Meg. Again, in 2011, you were—"

"Those were all religious rituals."

DCI Matthews snapped his notebook shut. "You would be advised to confine your religious rituals to daylight hours and to places where you have permission to go."

"My religion doesn't work like that," Richard said.

Lucas frowned at him. Talking back to a police officer was never a good idea.

"Does your religion tell you to go mucking about in murder scenes?" DCI Matthews asked in a level voice.

"We already explained what we were doing there," Lucas said.

"Yes, yes. Pacifying the spirits. Or you may have been returning to the scene of the crime."

Lucas tensed. "I have witnesses who can testify as to my whereabouts on the night of the murder."

"I have witnesses and CCTV footage to back me up," Richard said. "I was at the Knight Errant all night."

"Where were you on the night of May fifteenth?"

Lucas and Richard glanced at each other.

"Why?" Lucas asked.

"Because someone was found stabbed to death with their body dumped near Devil's Quoits stone circle up near Stanton Harcourt. The night was a full moon. I believe you people like that sort of thing, don't you?"

"The full moon has power, but nobody in the community engages in human sacrifice," Richard said. "Some of the Caribbean traditions sacrifice animals, but I don't do that. Blood isn't required for magic, so I've never seen any reason to spill it."

DCI Matthews narrowed his eyes. "You still haven't told me your whereabouts on that night."

"That was more than a month ago," Lucas said. "How are we supposed to remember? Would you remember without looking at your duty log?"

DCI Matthews stared at them for a moment. The silence drew out for several agonizing seconds. Lucas tried to maintain eye contact, a hard thing to do when you felt guilty as hell.

And what was this about another murder? The more he learned about this series of rituals, the worse it looked.

"What do you know about this case that you're not telling?" DCI Matthews asked.

"You mean what do we know that you'll believe?" Lucas asked.

"What's that supposed to mean?"

Lucas made a quick assessment of the policeman. This man was practical and despite his relatively young age seemed to have been around the block once or twice. Perhaps the same line that had worked (sort of) on Della would work (sort of) on this chap.

"I and Richard here are both students of the occult. We are familiar with various rituals and schools of magic. Wait, I see that look on your face. Before you dismiss me, let me tell you that I'm not expecting you to believe. But the people who put the human body parts in Wayland's Smithy certainly believe. If you want to catch them, you have to understand what's going on in their mind."

"Go on," policeman said, his face impassive.

"This ritual is intended to awaken the primate native forces of the land to fight foreigners. There is an unseemly subculture within occultism that has fallen for ultra-right-wing politics and white supremacy. They think by doing these rituals they can expel the foreign elements from this land. I wouldn't be at all surprised if, when you conduct a DNA analysis on those remains, that you find they are from an ethnic minority. I bet the person killed near the Devil's Quoits was a minority as well."

A slight twitch at the corner of DCI Matthews's mouth hinted that he had guessed right on both counts.

"So, what will be their next move?" DCI Matthews asked.

Lucas paused. Should he tell him about the ritual at the King Stone?

He decided not. If he did, the police would snoop around, asking Dr. Olding questions and finding no evidence. Doing that would put her and Whitaker on alert.

What about Alchester? No, that was a trap only he and Richard could lay.

And Della. He wondered how she was doing at that dinner from hell.

"Their idea is to perform a series of rituals to summon the traditional spirits of the land in order to eject what they see as invaders. They'll choose historical and archaeological sites that are associated with figures in folklore and legend."

"That's all of them," DCI Matthews grunted.

Lucas nodded. "Quite right. I would suggest

investigating occultists who have ties to right-wing groups." Realizing that might lead DCI Matthews astray, he quickly added, "The nature of the ritual shows that it is not Vigrid or any of the other well-known Nordic traditions. This group isn't so public in any case."

"We've been in occult circles for years, and we haven't heard of these people until now," Richard said. "Their style is completely new. I think they've been recruiting quietly and only recently started their activities."

"Can you give me any names?" DCI Matthews asked.

I can give you the names of a respected university professor and a millionaire. Somehow I don't think you'll accept those.

"No, I'm afraid not," Lucas said.

The policeman studied them for a moment longer, then stood.

"All right. I am releasing you on your own recognizance. You will be contacted about your court date. You can call a cab to get back to your vehicle."

"Thank you, Officer," Richard said. "If we hear anything through the grapevine that might be of help, we'll call you."

"You do that," DCI Matthews said, although he

did not look like he thought that would happen. "Here."

He handed each of them a card.

Lucas and Richard started to leave the room.

"And one more thing," DCI Matthews said.

They turned. The policeman's face was stern.

"If I catch either of you in any more criminal activity, it will mean a jail cell."

19

THE ROAST WAS DELICIOUS; the conversation terrifying.

Keaton Whitaker kept up a steady sales pitch. He talked about how impressed both he and Della's advisor were about her work, about all the projects he was going to fund, and how Della could go "very far, very far indeed" if she wanted to be a part of it all.

Dr. Olding remained silent through much of this, unusual for such an outspoken woman who was accustomed to being in charge. Della found it quite obvious who was the dominant one in this relation-ship. The professor kept giving Whitaker puppy-dog eyes like some little schoolgirl with a crush. Della found it nauseating.

Then Whitaker, no doubt feeling that he had softened up this eager American graduate student, got to what he really wanted.

"We have another excavation we're setting up in a couple of days, one which I think you could be of help with."

"A side project?" Della asked, looking at Dr. Olding, who gave her a flat smile. "I didn't think you would have the time."

Silently, she added, *I guess you do have the time now that you've found what you wanted at the King's Men.*

Dr. Olding leaned forward, still holding her fork with a bit of meat on the end.

"It's more along the lines of a survey. We want to take a look at Alchester."

"Where the sorcerer's disk came from? I'm surprised you got permission so quickly."

Not that you got permission at all. That doesn't bother you, though, does it?

Della tried to control her outrage. Dr. Olding was stealing artifacts, and now she wanted to excavate without permission. She was breaking all the basic ethics of her profession.

Small potatoes next to murder, Della told herself, but it still irked her.

"Oh, it's more a basic survey," her professor said. "We want to take a look around the surface of the site with fresh eyes." For some reason, that made Whitaker snicker. He tried to suppress it and hide behind his napkin, pretending to wipe his mouth, but Della heard. "We think there might be some features there that previous surveys and excavations missed."

"And we'd like you to come with us," Whitaker said. "You have quite the talent for finding hidden things."

"So, you want me to survey the site, and then you'll apply to excavate in the places I think are significant?"

Whitaker smiled. "Exactly."

Suddenly Della understood. Lucas's plan with the amulet was working. The plan had been to fool Dr. Olding and Whitaker into searching the site, thinking they had come across a place of great spiritual value. Lucas had said some nonsense about a counter spell. Della had ignored that. She had gone along with the idea because it could trick them into starting an illegal excavation. Della had no doubt that if she pointed out spots at Alchester, they would dig them the next night. She could call the police, these two would get busted, and the cops could hold them long enough to investigate the more serious crimes.

But her going along for the ride hadn't been part of the plan.

Della couldn't think of what to say, so Whitaker made up her mind for her.

"I'm very glad to have you on board with this. Cheers." He held up his wine glass.

"Cheers," Della mumbled, taking a sip of her own.

Whitaker switched to more general topics for the rest of the meal. He proved himself a scintillating conversationalist and did not dominate the conversation like so many successful men did. Della could understand why her professor had fallen for him, but after Dr. Olding learned his true nature, how could she still look at him with those loving eyes?

After dessert, Whitaker got up and drew back the curtain. Dr. Olding's moonlit back garden was vaguely visible through the glass.

"It's a lovely night, so nice after all this rain," he turned, making a poor show like he had suddenly had a brilliant idea. "How about we go out there tonight?"

"Tonight?" Dr. Olding said, as if surprised.

These two need to work on their acting skills, Della thought.

"Why not?" Whitaker said. "It's a beautiful night. We'll bring that white wine Della so kindly brought and go see the site in the moonlight."

"I don't think that will be a very scientific survey," Della said, plastering on a fake smile.

"Oh, but I disagree. To really know the land, you must see it in all lights. The Romans lived there in the night as well as the day, after all, and that great man who owned the amulet you found most certainly worked in the darkness."

That's the truest thing you've said all evening, Della thought. *Now think of a way out of this.*

"Well, it's been a wonderful evening. Thank you for dinner, Dr. Olding, but now I think—"

"Oh, it will be fun," Dr. Olding cut her off. "Keaton is always coming up with funny ideas like this."

"Show a little sense of adventure," Whitaker said with a grin. "We'll have a look at Alchester, drink some wine, and maybe see a couple of more sites of interest. Have you ever seen the King Stone or Iffley Grove under the moonlight? Stunning."

"Don't go anywhere with them."

Lucas's warning came back to her. As much nonsense as that man spouted, it was some damn good advice.

Dr. Olding put a hand on her arm. "Come along. It will be fun."

Della froze. Her mind raced, trying to think of excuses, but came up blank.

She opened her mouth, not knowing what would come out of it, and her phone rang.

Thank you, Lucas.

She pulled her phone out of her pocket.

It wasn't Lucas. It was Sebastian.

I'll take what I can get, Della thought, and picked up.

"Hey." Her ex-boyfriend sounded bereft. Guilty. Maybe even hungover. Good.

"Hey." Della said. She felt herself tense up. She didn't realize she could be any tenser than these two had already made her.

"I am so sorry. Can we talk?"

"Um, sure. I'm just finishing up dinner with my professor."

"Can I see you?" he asked, pleading.

"Sure. In an hour, you can come over to my

place." Her words came out harsh. She hung up without saying goodbye.

Dr. Olding and Whitaker glanced at each other.

"Everything all right?" Dr. Olding asked.

"It's my boyfriend. We had a fight. I'm sorry, but I need to go. Thank you for dinner."

Whitaker looked annoyed. Dr. Olding made sympathetic noises.

"I hope everything works out," Dr. Olding said as Della rose. "Oh, I have something I'd like to lend you."

Alarm bells went off in Della's head. Lucas had warned her not to accept anything.

Dr. Olding went to the front room, followed by Della and Whitaker. She searched through the volumes for a moment, pulled one off the shelf, and handed it to Della.

It was an old, leather-bound volume titled *The Spirit of Britain: Folklore and the Life of a People.* No author name appeared on the front cover.

Della opened it and saw no author name on the inside either, but it had a date from 1814.

"It's an excellent overview of how folklore has shaped our past and how we are as a people," Dr. Olding said. "Archaeologists tend to overlook folk-tales, but they give insight into the land. Read it when you get a chance."

Della hesitated. She couldn't think of a way to say no to borrowing a book. Besides, it was just a book, not a computer or something that could be electronically located. That was what had popped into her mind when Lucas had warned her not to accept anything. Really, the guy was worried about spells.

Well, spells were the one thing she didn't have to worry about. Della decided not to tell Lucas about it. A guy that unstable, with enough real things to worry about, didn't need the extra stress.

"Thank you. I'll take a look through it."

"I have a copy in my own library," Whitaker said. "A fascinating work. It was written during the Napoleonic Wars, when England was fighting for its very survival. We have different enemies now."

Della didn't know what to say to that. She managed a smile.

"Thank you for dinner."

Getting out of that house was a huge relief, quickly replaced by the stress of knowing she would have to meet Sebastian in a little while.

She trembled all the way home. Social situations were not her strong point. She'd always been shy, and situations with too many people or too much stress often overwhelmed her.

And in the past few days she had met a lunatic who thought he was a wizard, learned her boyfriend was gay and her professor was an occultist, and ate dinner with a pair of murderers.

Della fumbled with her keys at the front door, hurried up the stairs, ignoring the greeting from one of her neighbors walking down, entered her apartment, and slammed and locked the door behind her.

Shaking all over, she kicked off her shoes, walked across her apartment without bothering to turn on the lights, and collapsed on her bed. She wrapped a pillow around her head and closed her eyes, trying to block out the outside world.

All she wanted to do was hide. All she wanted to do was disappear.

A day. No, two. Just two days without any human contact or loud noises, and she'd feel all right again. No email. No phone. No television. Just books and silence. This had happened before, and she knew what she needed.

After many minutes, the shaking receded. Della's breathing reduced to a normal rate. The iron grip of tension began to ease. She was a long way from fine, but a solid eight hours of sleep would help.

Then two days off. She'd speak to no one. The hell with Dr. Olding and Lucas and graduate school and all the rest. She could make up excuses later.

Her door buzzer rang.

Oh, God.

For a moment she'd forgotten all about Sebastian. She'd like to continue forgetting about him.

She ignored the buzzer, hoping he'd go away.

It buzzed a few more times before stopping.

She let out a breath of relief.

Then her phone rang.

"Damn it!"

She leapt up and pulled the phone from her pocket.

"What?" she demanded.

"I'm here," Sebastian said, abashed.

"Come back in an hour."

She hung up, immediately feeling sorry. Being snappy and bossy didn't come naturally to her. She put her phone on silent, got into her pajamas, and buried herself under the covers even though it was far too early to sleep.

Della forced herself to breathe slowly and relax her muscles one by one. She'd taken an online meditation course to try and control her anxiety levels. It worked if she focused on it, sort of. She only wished it worked all the time. When she got like this, any little thing could set her off.

She was just beginning to feel partway to normal when the buzzer rang again.

"Ugh!"

She looked at her phone. Sebastian had waited precisely an hour. The idiot had probably been standing on the other side of the street staring at his watch.

Grumbling a string of curse words, she turned on the lights in her apartment. Sebastian buzzed again.

"I'm coming!" she snapped, although of course he couldn't hear her.

She stomped over to her door and buzzed him in.

His regular tread sounded on the stairs. When it reached her landing, she opened the door.

Sebastian stood there, eyes rimmed in red, a bouquet of roses in one hand and a bottle of wine in the other.

In fact, the exact same vintage as the one she had brought to Dr. Olding's house earlier that evening.

She burst out laughing. Sebastian paled, looking distraught, and that only made her laugh harder. He must have played through in his mind all the possible reactions she'd have to seeing him again, and laughing out loud had definitely not made the list.

Still laughing, with a high note of hysteria cutting her voice, she said, "Come on in."

"Are you... all right?" Sebastian asked.

That got her laughing harder. A part of her mind, the part that always remained a bit detached from the world, did not like the way she was acting.

"Not even close," she admitted.

"I am so sorry."

The laughter cut off, sharp. Suddenly nothing was funny anymore.

She jabbed a finger in his direction, "You are the least of my worries right now, believe me."

"What's wrong?"

Oh God, the Concerned Sensitive Guy look, Della thought. *I used to find that endearing.*

"Let's just say that work has been a wee bit stressful."

Sebastian stood in the middle of her living room, still holding the flowers and wine.

"I'm sorry," he said.

"I think you mentioned that. There's a spare vase on the kitchen counter. Put the flowers in it with some water. The wine can go in the fridge. I've drunk enough tonight. Or maybe I haven't drunk enough. I don't know, but I sure as hell don't want to drink with you."

Sebastian slumped into the kitchen while Della collapsed on the couch.

Don't apologize. Don't apologize.

"Sorry for snapping at you."

Crap.

"It's my fault," he said from the kitchen.

"Not entirely."

"So, what's going wrong with work? Did you find out more about what your professor was up to the other night?"

She was about to let it all pour out but caught herself at the last moment.

"Please, let's keep this between ourselves," Lucas had told her. *"Your boyfriend knows too much already. He's just an innocent bystander."*

Sebastian came out of the kitchen.

"Did you sleep with any of them?" she asked.

It was a good way to change the subject, and it was what she really wanted to know anyway.

"No," he said, sitting down on an armchair opposite her. "Despite appearances, my hypocrisy has its limits."

Della spread out her arms. "But why? Why date me? And why not tell me? I told you about my cousin. I wasn't going to judge you."

Sebastian grimaced. "It's a bit hard to explain."

"Try me."

Sebastian let out a sigh. "I'm bi. I think. I like you. I find women attractive. I like our cuddles and our evenings together, but more and more I'm thinking of... other things. I was wondering if it was just a phase. You see, at school I and another lad experimented a bit. I developed quite the crush on him, but he only saw it all as a lark. When I pursued him, he told everyone I was queer. That got me the attention of some of the school bullies. I never mentioned just how Donald knew I was queer. It didn't seem fair."

"I'm glad you didn't stoop down to his level."

"I was tempted, trust me. So, after that I made a point of dating as many girls as possible. It quashed the rumors eventually, but I never forgot that my first time was with a boy."

"And you've been in the closet ever since?"

"More or less, yes."

Della frowned. "And when you were with me was it more or less?"

Sebastian shifted in his seat. He hadn't looked at her once during the entire conversation. "Less, but then it became more. I... realized that my physical desire for you was lacking and that I kept thinking about the Knight Errant. Every time I saw an advert for it, I started obsessing about it."

"How long have you been going there?"

"A little over a month. All I did was dance and talk to people. It felt so liberating just being there. I didn't have to tell anyone anything. They all just assumed. It was so easy, no natural. I'm sorry, it's not your fault. It was wretched to do something like that to you. I should have broken up with you instead of been a sneak behind your back. But I never cheated on you."

"Slow dancing with a dude doesn't count as cheating?"

Sebastian flushed, then looked at her. "What were you doing there?"

"None of your business. In fact, nothing I do is any of your business anymore. Please leave."

"But—"

"Go. I'm not blaming you for coming out, but you should have left me before running around with guys. I can't have a relationship based on dishonesty."

"I'd still like to be your friend, Della." Sebastian was on the verge of tears.

"I can't be friends with someone I can't trust. You know how hard relationships are for me. I've talked with you about it. And then you pull a stunt like this? Please leave."

Sebastian got up and moved to the door.

"I'm sorry."

"So am I. Now go," Della said, cursing herself when she heard her voice crack.

She just managed to push him out of the door and slam it behind him before she started bawling.

20

ALL LUCAS WANTED to do was to curl up in a ball and hide, but Della wasn't checking her phone, and he needed to find out what was going on with her. After dropping off an exhausted Richard, he drove over to Della's house and buzzed her flat. No answer.

"Damn it."

He tried calling her. She didn't pick up.

Confused, he looked around the street and recognized Della's car parked nearby. Why the hell didn't she answer? It was too early to go to bed.

He buzzed again, leaning on the ringer.

"Go away!" Della's voice shrieked through the intercom.

"It's me."

Long pause.

The door clicked open.

Lucas climbed the stairs. Della appeared at the top, her eyes red and her makeup a mess.

"What happened to you?" she asked.

Lucas still had the bandage wrapped around his head and a big bruise on one cheek.

"Long story. And you?"

"Nothing," Della mumbled.

"Sorry to disturb you. This is obviously a bad time, but things are getting serious."

"Come on in," she sighed.

"Are you all right?" he asked. "What happened at dinner?"

"I'm fine. No, I'm not. I don't know. You want some tea?"

"That would be lovely."

Lucas sat in the living room and gave Della some space. He could hear her moving around the kitchen. She didn't speak to him.

After a minute, she came out with two steaming cups. She curled up on the far end of the sofa and buried her face in the steam rising from her cup, inhaling the delicate fragrance of pekoe.

"Tell me everything," Lucas said.

In terse words with little elaboration, Della ran

through the events of the evening. The dinner at Dr. Olding's house had gone more or less as Lucas had expected. Keaton Whitaker was there, and they had tried to recruit her with a mixture of flattery and bribes. A soft sell. One doesn't just come out and ask one's graduate student to join a cult.

More seriously, they had tried to get her to go to Alchester.

"At that point I knew I had to get out of there," she said. "No way I was going anywhere after dark with them. I was trying to make up excuses, but they started putting on the pressure. You wouldn't believe who saved me."

"Sebastian?"

She smiled bitterly. "How did you guess? The makeup streaks all down my face?"

"That was a bit of a hint, yes."

She shook her head sadly and took another sip of her tea. "You know, he didn't tell me anything Richard hadn't already warned me about. He was all contrite and guilty and everything he should be, but simply seeing him was too much. This whole thing has been too much. I'm a quiet person, Lucas. I don't like drama, and I sure as hell don't like this much drama all at once. I can't take this."

"But you have. You walked into a house with two

murderers and managed to have dinner without panicking. You're stronger than you think."

"Don't feel like it," she mumbled into her tea. Then she looked up. "So, what's your story?"

"Not one you're going to believe."

But he told her anyway, every last bit of it.

By the time he started talking about entering Wayland's Smithy with Richard, his hand was shaking so much he had to put the teacup down.

When he reached the part about the candles blowing out, his words came out in sobs.

Bile rose in his throat. His stomach churned. He rushed to the bathroom and made it to the toilet in the nick of time.

Lucas puked the remains of his supper, gripping the bowl as he shivered with a cold sweat.

Dimly he noticed Della's hand on his shoulder and her saying all those concerned, supportive, and ultimately useless words people said when someone went past their limit.

He finished emptying his stomach, then sat down on the cold tile for a minute in case there was more to come. Della gave him some toilet paper to wipe his mouth, followed by a shot of Listerine.

Lucas managed a weak smile. "Thank you. The

last time I needed this treatment was after a pub crawl with Richard."

"Not a good idea to have him as a drinking partner," she said, smiling back. She sat on the edge of the tub. "So, tell me the rest."

He shuddered. "First I should tell you what happened to my parents, because it was more than this that has me on the floor right now."

"Your parents? Are they dead? I'm sorry."

Lucas rubbed his temples. "I'm sorry too, and I don't even know if they're dead. They were both major occultists, important in the field. That earned them enemies. There's no shortage of jealous, petty people in occultism. I don't know who they crossed, but they must have angered someone important. No doubt they tried to stop some evil ritual like we are. Someone sent a spirit after me."

"Someone sent a devil after you?"

He shook his head. "There are no devils, not in the way you think. The Christian cosmology is far too simplistic to describe the compLucas network of forces in the universe. But yes, they sent some dark being after me in my bedroom. I was only nine. I screamed bloody murder when I saw it, and my parents rushed in. They saved me but got taken in my place."

Lucas fought back tears, cleared his throat, and continued.

"The disappearance of two important occultists made headlines, of course. The gutter press besieged the house. They even faked photos of ghosts at my window. My aunt and uncle took me in, fought off the papers until they found a new flavor of the month, feigned ignorance to the police, and raised me as their own. And now, at Wayland's Smithy, I got attacked by another spirit, one raised by a cult very much like the one that took my parents. I thought I could stay away from all this. It looks like it won't let me."

As he spoke, Lucas saw Della's face go from concerned to guarded to borderline frightened. He had seen that look before. It was the look of a nonbeliever gauging your sanity and finding it wanting. He squared his shoulders. Enough mucking about. He needed this girl's help, and he didn't give a damn what she believed.

"So that's what we're up against," he said once he'd finished. "You still onside for trapping them at Alchester?"

"They're murderers," Della said. Lucas knew that was the only reason she was helping out and that she did not for a moment believe the magical aspect of it. Still, she deserved to know, even if it made her look at him as if he were a candidate for Bedlam.

"Yes, they are murderers," Lucas said as he got to his feet. "And they're only starting their killing spree."

"They wanted to go there tonight. What if they're there now?"

Lucas washed his face at the sink. "They want to go with you. We'll fix it up. Besides, I can't take any more tonight."

Della hugged herself. "Neither can I."

She gave him a washcloth, and he dried his face, feeling better. "I should go. We're both exhausted."

"Can I stay at your place?"

The question caught him by surprise. "Excuse me?"

"I... don't want to be here if Sebastian comes back. And the department has my address. It wouldn't be hard for Dr. Olding to get that."

"Good point. All right. We have a spare room. I think you'll like my aunt and uncle. And I know they're interested in meeting you."

Della packed and then drove behind him as they made their way out of Oxford and through the countryside.

The lights were still on in the main house when

they drove up. By the time they got out of their cars, the front door was open, and the familiar silhouettes of his aunt and uncle stood in the doorway. Lucas almost sobbed with relief.

"What happened?" his aunt asked before he even had a chance to introduce Della. "I felt it all the way from here."

"Long story, Auntie. This is Della, as you might have guessed."

Aunt Mary gave him a concerned look before turning to Della.

"You look knackered. I'll go put the kettle on."

Della smiled a little. "The English solution to everything."

"Come on in," Uncle Philip said. "We'll sit in the library. I'm sure Mary will be rummaging through the books soon enough."

Della left her bag in the front hall, and they passed through to the library. She stopped and stared in wonder at the ornate old room and all the books in it.

"Pretty impressive, isn't it?" Uncle Philip said. "Feel free to have a browse. Lucas, let me take a look at those bumps."

Lucas sat, and his uncle expertly examined his wounds.

"My uncle was a physician for the Red Cross for many years," Lucas explained as Della walked slowly along one of the shelves, reading the titles. "He spent much of his career in war zones such as Bosnia and Rwanda."

"Tending sheep is a bit more relaxing," Uncle Philip. "This is an impressive bump you got here. I'm waiting for the story behind it."

"You'll have to wait for Aunt Mary first. How are you doing over there, Della?"

"Your aunt has quite the library," she said, although her voice sounded restrained. Her mouth made a prim line. She had pulled a grimoire off the shelf and read the title. *"The Demons of the Fifth Circle of Hades, Their Summoning and Banishment.* Sounds charming."

"More of a metaphorical work," Lucas said. "That was published in 1689. Back then, many practitioners were still influenced by hostile church teachings and thought demons were literally true."

"I thought you were attacked by a demon tonight," Della said. Despite all she had been through, she laced her words with sarcasm. This girl was nothing if not relentless in her skepticism, Lucas mused. Too much time in the classroom.

"I was attacked by a focused manifestation of the *genius loci*."

"Oh, now it all makes sense."

Uncle Philip chuckled, patting Lucas on the shoulder, and whispered, "Sounds like when me and your auntie were courting."

"Instead of annoying remarks, may I have a whiskey?"

"Not after a head injury. Ah, here's the tea!"

Everyone sat and got themselves comfortable. Aunt Mary gave Della a warm smile as she served the tea.

"From what Lucas tells me, you've been through the wringer in the past few days, and I am sure you are confused and doubtful about what is going on. Be assured you're perfectly safe here. How about you tell me what happened tonight."

Della and Lucas both told their stories. Aunt Mary looked grim. So did Lucas's uncle, although he had less of an understanding of just how serious the situation was.

Lucas finished up with what he had learned from the unlikely source of DCI Matthews.

"Apparently someone was murdered on the last full moon over at the Devil's Quoits. The inspector didn't say, but I gather he or she was a foreigner. So, this ritual has been going on for longer than we suspected. I don't understand why they picked that spot. There's no proper legend associated with it, at least not one connected to a famous practitioner or pagan god."

"What is the legend?" Della asked.

"That the Devil met a beggar one night and made a wager with him. They'd play quoits, and if the beggar won, he'd be a rich man. If the Devil won, he'd take the beggar's soul. They stood on top of Wytham Hill a few miles away and tossed the quoits. The Devil used the stones of the circle and hurled them all the way to the present location. He won, of course, and took the man's soul." Lucas turned to his aunt. "But the Devil doesn't exist, so what's the *genius loci*? What are they tapping into?"

"Evil. The loss of humanity. The loss of hope. They are putting a malevolent flavor onto any further rituals they perform. It's an initial ritual, one to strengthen the ones that come later on. The ritual Della stumbled onto was the first proper ritual. The sacrifice at the Devil's Quoits was only the preparation."

"What a preparation," Lucas said, turning pale. "So, what do we do?"

Aunt Mary thought for a moment. At last she spoke.

"Your plan to trap them at Alchester is still the best one. Richard will be a great help. Is he still up to the challenge?"

"More so than ever, Auntie."

"Good man. You could learn a lot from him, Lucas."

Lucas smiled. "I'm not sure I want to learn all he would like to teach me."

Aunt Mary looked helplessly at Della. "See what I have to contend with? You're more cooperative than he is, and you don't even believe."

Della shifted in her seat. "Well, I don't mean to criticize your beliefs. All spiritual traditions have some merit and ..."

Aunt Mary raised a hand. "Spare me the political correctness. You think this is all tosh, and that's perfectly all right. I've heard it all before from more people than I dare count. I don't hold it against them. I even married one of them. Anyway, as I was saying, you should go ahead with the Alchester plan. Della, you say they asked you to visit the site. You were quite right not to go in the darkness, but how about you volunteer to go out there with them after work tomorrow?"

Della groaned.

"I can't," she said. "I'm sorry, but I just can't. It's all been too much. I need a day or two to—"

"In a day or two, more people will get killed," Aunt Mary said.

Della slumped.

"What do I have to do?"

"Go through your day as normal. Late in the afternoon, suggest to Dr. Olding that you visit Alchester after work. She'll go with you, and Whitaker will probably come along too. Then point out a couple of spots you find 'interesting.' It doesn't matter where, just point to something. Preferably something close enough to some cover that you, my nephew, and Richard can hide and get a good view of what's going on. Because they will most certainly come back after dark to check it out."

"And they'll dig on an archaeological site illegally," Della said.

"Yes."

"Fine," Della said with a note of resignation. "That's all we need to arrest them."

Lucas felt guilty misleading her into thinking that was all they'd see. If she was this overwrought after what little she had already been through, how would she be after tomorrow night?

Aunt Mary smiled. "Now I think we all need a good night's rest. The guest bedroom is up the stairs, second door on the left. Why don't you go to bed?"

"Thank you. I'm exhausted."

As Della left the room, Lucas leaned over to Aunt Mary and said in a low voice, "Do you think you could do something for her? She's really at the end of her tether."

"I've already put certain amulets in the guest bedroom. They'll calm her. I'll do a ritual as well. It will soothe the negative thoughts and give her peace of mind."

"A ritual for peace of mind? Why haven't you done that for me?"

Aunt Mary looked at him sadly.

"I've been doing it every day for twenty years."

21

DELLA DRAGGED her bag to the guest bedroom. All she wanted to do was sleep until this whole thing went away. The craziness with her boss and with Sebastian, it was all too much.

Now Della had another problem on her hands. At first she had dismissed Lucas as a crank, then as an intelligent but deluded person. Now she could see he was mentally ill. Whatever intruder had killed his parents had been turned into a nightmare creature and populated his psyche with occult monsters. She pitied him.

At least she didn't fear him. Despite all the crazy ideas in his head and the rituals he performed, Lucas was harmless. He was a victim and could never be a perpetrator.

But how could she help him? He was surrounded by people who enabled his delusions—Richard, his aunt, even his uncle played along, although Della sensed he didn't really believe. Lucas had built a world around himself that fed his mental illness.

Della wondered if she was the only person in his life who confronted him on this stuff.

A soft knock came on her door. Della opened it.

Philip stood there with some towels. "Brought these for you. Do you need anything else?"

"No, thanks. You've been very kind."

"Sleep in as long as you like. Your boss won't snap at you for being late. She needs you too much."

"And here I thought she liked me because I was a good archaeology student."

Philip smiled. "You think she's bonkers, don't you?"

"Look, I—"

"Don't worry about it. I didn't believe for years. There are parts I still don't believe. But that didn't stop me and Mary from having a strong relationship. Lucas is a good lad. He won't steer you wrong."

"Um, thanks." Della said, wondering what he meant by that. It almost sounded like a setup.

Della closed the door, got undressed, and fell asleep before her head hit the pillow.

She woke up ten hours later, opening her eyes to sunlight streaming through lace curtains and the mingled sound of birdsong and bleating sheep. The sun was high in the sky. She was very late for work and somehow didn't care at all. A soothing calm enveloped her like a warm duvet.

For a moment she lay there, utterly relaxed. If she felt a bit confused that she should feel so serene despite what had happened in the last few days, she didn't dwell on it. The way forward was clear now.

The smell of bacon finally roused her. Della sat and surveyed the room. The previous night, she was so tired she hadn't even seen it.

The room was small and filled with perfectly preserved antique furniture. On the walls were old prints of castles and stone circles. The corner table held a shrine with a large reproduction of the Venus of Willendorf, a plump female figure carved in the Paleolithic some thirty thousand years ago. Before it were incense sticks, a tray of colorful river stones, and some bits of fossilized wood.

Della smiled at the mixture of archaeology and superstition. It seemed appropriate to the circumstances.

Following the smell downstairs to the kitchen, she found Lucas cooking up breakfast at an antique iron stove.

"Sleep well?" he asked over his shoulder.

"Like a log."

"So did I. There's bacon and eggs for breakfast. You're not vegan, are you?"

"No."

"Good. We raise sheep. If you stay for dinner, we'll cook you up some freshly slaughtered mutton."

"Sounds tasty, but we have a job to do tonight."

"We do indeed."

They ate in silence. Not until they were almost finished did Della realize she hadn't checked her phone first thing upon waking up. This old house with its antiques seemed out of time. She hadn't seen a television or even a radio around.

Della supposed she should check her messages. Surely there would be one from Dr. Olding asking where she was. Della shrugged off the idea. Her professor needed her and would tolerate her absence if she came through by going to Alchester. Della had power over her. That gave Della a smug sense of satisfaction.

"This place is very relaxing," Della observed as she helped Lucas wash up.

"A bit of my aunt's magic."

"More like it's rural quiet and has good decor."

Lucas chuckled. "Um, yes, that's it exactly."

"Where are they?"

"My uncle is out in the fields. My aunt is in the library working. And you best be going to the dig."

Della felt a tug of regret leaving this place. It felt like a refuge. As odd as the residents were, they were kind. She went upstairs, showered and changed, and finally checked her messages.

There was only a text from Dr. Olding, from about an hour before.

"Is everything all right? I hope there wasn't too much trouble last night."

Oh right, she had used Sebastian as an excuse. At least he was good for something.

She texted back that she was heading to the dig.

When she got there, it was almost time for lunch. Dr. Olding greeted her, and she got to work on her square. No one bothered her. Obviously the news had gotten around that she was having some guy trouble.

That suited her just fine. She needed some space and worked quietly for the rest of the day, slowly uncovering two Bronze Age cinerary urns. Dr.

Olding was right in her prediction that the cemetery extended to this new square. A shame that such a capable archaeologist had fallen into some seriously bad ways.

Near the end of the day, Dr. Olding came over to her square. Now was the time.

"Looks like those urns are coming out well," her professor said as she crouched down beside her. "I notice there's a hairline crack on that one. Be careful as you dig down. If it starts getting unstable, we'll have to pull it out before it collapses and spills the content."

"I'll keep an eye out. Sorry for being late today."

"Not a problem. I hope everything works out between you two."

"How about I make it up to you? Let's go out to Alchester after work."

Dr. Olding brightened. "That's a great idea. What a pity Keaton can't make it. He has a meeting all afternoon. He's desperately busy with a new contract for the Department of Defense."

Relief washed over Della when she heard this. Smiling, she said, "Well, maybe I can come up with some things that will give him a pleasant surprise after a long work day."

Oh, we're going to surprise you, all right, Della thought.

Half an hour later, everyone packed up for the day. Dr. Olding got in her car, and Della followed her in her own for the forty minutes it took to get to Bicester.

They parked in the little parking lot of a Norman-style church with an imposing square tower and a cemetery filled with mossy gravestones.

"It's this way," Dr. Olding said, indicating an open, grassy field behind the church.

Della blinked. She hadn't realized it was so close to town. The church was on a little side street just off a road lined on both sides with shops and houses, several of which were visible from the parking lot. Once they entered the cemetery, they went out of sight behind a hedge, but the field beneath which Alchester lay was clearly visible. Besides the cemetery and a few trees, there was barely any cover at all. Beyond the field, which stretched about three hundred meters, Della spotted more houses and a playground. Small children played on a seesaw and jungle gym while their parents doted on them. Other parents didn't dote. They sat on a park bench nearby, texting.

Sneaking up on the cult tonight would be tricky.

Della followed her professor through the grave-yard, hopped a little stream that ran behind it, and strolled onto the field.

While no ruins stood above ground, Della's trained eyes immediately noticed that this was an archaeological site. The level ground was disturbed here and there by low mounds and rills, telltale signs of stone structures beneath. As they walked farther into the field, she began to pick out shapes—rectangles and squares, the foundations of Roman buildings that had fallen down 1,600 or more years ago.

"Wow," Della whispered, her wonder at the site temporarily overcoming her fear of the situation. "I think we're on the main road here."

Dr. Olding nodded. "You have a good eye, just like Keaton and I said. You've spotted that there are structures to either side and nothing in a strip going that way. This is just a municipal road. There's a couple of more major roads connecting the old towns. Some people like going for country walks on them. They're plainly visible in parts because they were covered in small stones back in the Roman times. You can still see them as clear strips through the woodland."

"Remarkable," Della said. "I think I need to get out of the library and the lab more."

"It's not a bad idea. An archaeologist needs to know the land, as does anyone who loves their country and wants to protect it. But you've already been on a Roman road. Part of the A41 follows an old Roman road, the same one that connected Alchester with other Roman towns."

Della shook her head in wonder. That was the highway they had used to get here.

She began to move around the low humps that were once Roman homes and barracks and baths. Dr. Olding watched her expectantly.

Della took her time, wanting to heighten the suspense. If this fool thought she had magical powers that would find ancient artifacts, she'd give her a bit of a show.

She moved a little away from her professor in the direction of the church and the trees. A large bush at the end of the cemetery, where there was also a cluster of larger gravestones, should give her and Lucas something to hide behind. She picked a spot about fifty or sixty meters away from the gravestone clusters that would be clearly visible from that vantage point.

"Hm, this spot is interesting," she murmured, as if to herself.

Her professor rushed up to her. "Really? How so?"

Della waved her hand vaguely over the low mound that looked like a thick retaining wall for some large structure.

"Oh, I don't know. Just a feeling." She let out a laugh. "Hardly scientific, I know, but I get a feeling for things sometimes. You know, just before digging up that sorcerer's medallion I could have sworn I was on the brink of an interesting discovery? It was like I knew it was there."

"Interesting." Dr. Olding's response was noncommittal, her face a mask, but Della knew she was lapping it all up. She could see it in her eyes. If it weren't for the fact that she was speaking to a murderer, she would have burst out laughing.

Della walked about ten meters to her left and stared intently at a spot on the ground. She worried that she might be hamming it up a bit too much, but Dr. Olding took the bait. When she next looked at her professor, she saw she had pulled a handheld scientific GPS device accurate down to a few centimeters. She noted the location where they had talked, then hurried over to where Della stood and noted that spot down as well.

A man walked his dog onto the field not far from them.

Damn, this is really exposed. We have to be careful tonight.

"A fascinating place," Della said. "Gets me all tingly."

"Does it now?" Dr. Olding said, watching the dog-walker pass by.

"Oh yes. You can feel the history here. I'm glad they've left this unplowed."

"Aerial photography discovered the site some decades ago," her professor said. "Since then it's been pasture land. There have been a few excavations but none recently. Shall we look around a bit more?"

Della allowed Dr. Olding to walk around the field with her as she explained what was found in previous excavations on the site. What began as an Iron Age settlement was initially conquered during the invasion by the emperor Claudius, whose army built a fort at the spot. The fort was later expanded as Roman control over the region grew. Soon the town of Alchester sprang up to serve both the fort and the trade moving along two major Roman roads that intersected nearby. Eventually, the *Pax*

Romana had extended enough over the land that the fort was abandoned, but the town continued to thrive until the Roman legions left the declining province in 410 AD to protect the heart of the Roman Empire in the face of continual pressure from its enemies.

"But by then it was too late," her professor said, shaking her head. "The Romans had let in too many barbarians, allowing foreigners to gain positions of power and letting large foreign populations settle within the boundaries of the empire. The Romans had lost their sense of self and lost the will and organization to resist the pressure on the borders. Within a couple of years, the barbarians sacked Rome and within a couple of generations overthrew the last emperor. It was all over after that. One of the greatest civilizations the world has ever seen died out, all in the name of tolerance and multiculturalism."

"I don't think the Romans used those terms," Della snapped, unable to restrain herself. "Or thought that way."

Dr. Olding smiled. "No, I suppose they didn't. But look at the result. The Romans should have kept Rome for the Romans. Who knows how long their empire might have lasted, and now all we have is this barren field and the legacy they have left us. Any more spots of interest?"

Della shrugged. Throughout their walk she had glanced back at the two spots she had indicated, as if she felt a strange pull toward them. She had made sure Dr. Olding noticed.

"No," she said, glancing back at them again. "This has been very interesting, though. You can feel the history in this place."

That much, at least, was true. Della felt bad that she was encouraging Dr. Olding and her companions to do an illegal dig on this spot, but it was necessary if she wanted to stop these murderers.

Some things were more important than archaeology.

Dr. Olding turned to her. "So, are you all right? It's not like you to be late for work. You said you had an argument with your boyfriend."

"Ex-boyfriend now."

Dr. Olding held her hand. Della had to use all her willpower not to pull away.

"I'm sorry to hear that," her professor said.

"Yeah, so am I."

"What happened?"

Della looked at her. Her professor had never

spoken of personal matters before, and Della certainly didn't want her to start now.

"I don't really want to talk about it."

Dr. Olding squeezed her hand. "Don't worry. You're young, and there are plenty of good guys out there. It just takes some time to find them. You know I was married for fifteen years?"

"Really?"

"Yes, to another academic. An economics professor. We started out well until my career took off and his faltered. He got jealous, and things began to sour between us. A lot of men can't handle being with a more successful woman."

"Where is he now?"

"A nowhere university. From what I hear, after he left me, he threw himself into work. It doesn't seem to have done much good. I thought he was the right one. Turned out I was wrong. I've found the right one now. It took until my early fifties, but I finally found him."

"Mr. Whitaker?"

Della really didn't want to have a heart-to-heart with this nutcase, but it might turn up some interesting information, though.

"Oh, call him Keaton. He doesn't sit on formalities. That's one of the things I love about him."

Della couldn't believe how smitten her professor looked. Was this how Whitaker got her to go against her professional ethics? Sweep her off her feet? Della felt disappointed. Such an intelligent, successful woman falling for the wrong man.

Well, hadn't she done that too?

At least Sebastian wasn't a killer. Just confused, immature, and selfish. Perhaps she had been too hard on him. She still felt guilty kicking him out of her apartment like that. She reminded herself to get her spare set of keys back from him. Perhaps they could have a brief conversation, and she could smooth things over a bit.

Della realized that it was her turn to talk.

"Mr. Whitaker is certainly not going to be insecure about success," she said to fill the awkward silence.

Dr. Olding laughed. "Oh no, he's got moneybags. What's nice, though, is that he respects me for what I do. He's always been fascinated by the past, and I think he's a little bit envious that I get to excavate all day while he's sitting in a boardroom. He calls it the 'bored room.' Get it? I've had to deal with many wealthy patrons in my career, and most are always slightly condescending. He's never been that way. He always treats me with respect. Generous too."

Dr. Olding reached beneath her work shirt and pulled on a gold chain to reveal a large white orb at the end of it. The orb was about the size of an eye, pearly white, with a brown circle inset with a brilliant diamond that glittered in the sunlight.

"I've never seen a stone like that before." Della found it oddly beautiful, although at the same time a bit unsettling. She wasn't sure why she felt that way.

"It's called an eyestone. It's a little-known style of jewelry from the ancient Germanic cultures. Very, very few people these days know how to fashion one."

"What kind of gem is that? It looks like a pearl except that it's too big."

"Oh, it isn't a gem. Or at least it wasn't one until the process was complete. Do you like it?"

Dr. Olding twisted it a little in the sunlight, and the diamond at the center of the brown ring flashed and sparkled. Della stared at it and got the strange feeling that it was staring back.

As if from a great distance she heard her professor speaking.

"I do hope that you will consider our offer, Della. You have a remarkable talent. You could go very far. Very far. Read that book I lent you. Don't forget to read the book, Della. It's very important.

Very important. You should read it tonight. Yes, read it tonight."

When Della drove home a few minutes later, her mind felt blurry, as if shrouded in a thick fog. She had trouble recalling exactly what was said between her and her professor as they were leaving, but she knew she had a bit of time before having to meet Lucas and Richard.

Time to herself.

Time to do some reading.

22

NO MATTER what sort of situation in which he spent time with Richard, Lucas always seemed to end up in a pub.

Even when staking out a murderous cult intent on wiping out every non-English person in the country, he found himself at a small table with a pint in his hand. It was his first of the evening. Richard was on his third. The chap was pacing himself because of the seriousness of the work at hand.

Della was having a mineral water. Such spoilsports, the Americans.

"So, run this by me again," she said, keeping her voice low despite the boisterous early evening crowd.

Lucas was taken aback. They had gone over this

before. Della seemed distracted tonight, quite unlike her usual sharp self. Must be that damned boyfriend. What terrible timing for all that to happen right when they needed her to help out with catching this cult.

"Quite simple," Lucas said. "This pub is well situated on the main entrance to town. We sit here until we see Dr. Olding's car pass. No doubt the others will be coming through one by one so as not to attract attention. Some might have gone by already. When we spot her, we give them another half hour to get set up, and then we go take a look."

"And if they're digging, we call the police," Della said.

"Let's not get ahead of ourselves. They will do a ritual with the amulet you planted, a ritual to summon the spirit of the long-dead sorcerer. They think that because they have his amulet that they will be able to control him like Mother Shipton and Wayland the Smith, but the amulet is a fake."

Richard leaned forward and joined the conversation. "The summoning will work. They're certainly capable of that, but they need the correct amulet to control the spirit. A bit like how in more traditional summonings, the practitioner uses a pentagram. The spirit will be unrestrained, always a dangerous proposition, and it will grow angrier when it tastes the flavor of the magic they are attempting."

"And why will this be a grumpy ghost?" Della asked, not taking her eyes off the damp street outside. Every minute or so, a car or truck passed under the nearby streetlight, clearly visible despite a gathering mist.

"Don't be condescending," Richard said. "The spirit will object to the nature of the spell they want him to help with because the original sorcerer was Egyptian."

Della rolled her eyes. "And how the hell can you know that?"

Lucas smiled. All right, perhaps she was becoming more of herself again, although she seemed oddly eager for all this to start when before she was justifiably reluctant. When they had first met at the pub that evening, Della grumbled something about being taken away from her reading. How could someone read at a time like this?

"Egyptian sorcerers were in high demand in the Roman Empire and could be found in all the provinces," Lucas told her. "The first clue we had of his origin was the crocodile head on the figure in the amulet."

Lucas pulled out the amulet, the real one. He

would need this tonight.

If only he had the capability to wield it properly.

"Yes, Sobek," Della said. "Dr. Olding mentioned it when I pulled it out of the ground. But just because he was using Egyptian symbolism doesn't mean the guy was Egyptian."

Lucas glanced at Richard, who smiled into his pint glass.

"Well, we do know he was Egyptian because my aunt"—Lucas cleared his throat—"talked to him."

Della uttered some very unladylike words under her breath. Otherwise, she didn't reply.

Lucas's heart sank. He knew that she'd never believe all this, but he wanted to at least try. Her belief was becoming important to him. Not only because it would help with the task at hand but because it would be nice to have at least one person in his life who wasn't involved with magic who didn't laugh at him about it.

It looked like she would keep on laughing.

"So, when do we call the cops?" she asked.

We don't, Lucas thought. *We won't have to.*

"As soon as we see them do something illegal," he told her.

"If this mist gets any worse, we won't see them do a damn thing." Suddenly, she perked up. "That was Dr. Olding's car that just passed."

"Are you sure?" Lucas asked.

"Of course. I see it every day. Oh hey, I think that's Whitaker's car."

A vintage Jaguar passed by.

"All right, let's sit tight;" Richard said. "We're going to need to wait for them to set up. Anyone want another pint?"

"God no," Della said. "And haven't you had enough?"

"Girl, do I look drunk to you?"

Della rolled her eyes. Richard went to the bar and came back with three drinks—pints for him and Lucas and a margarita that he put in front of Della.

"I told you I didn't want a drink," the archaeology student said.

"Don't worry honey, it's a virgin margarita." Richard put on a face of mock concern. "Wait. You aren't, are you? They might try to sacrifice you."

"Not funny," Della said, blushing. Then she started to giggle.

Lucas and Richard looked at her with concern. That giggle was hysterical, not humorous.

"You all right?" Richard asked.

"Absolutely not," Della griped.

The next half hour seemed to take days. Both Lucas and Della kept looking at their phones. Only Richard sat there calmly, lost in his own thoughts.

Lucas wondered about him. His friend still wore his bandages, as did Lucas. If things went wrong tonight, Richard would get the worst of it, and yet he was the most composed. Despite his outward silliness, the man had inner reservoirs of strength Lucas could only guess at.

Perhaps I should study more, Lucas thought. *It looks like I can't avoid magic. It keeps coming up in my life.*

At last the time came.

They left the pub and entered a thickening mist that made the streetlights a hazy glow and turned the buildings and pedestrians into indistinct shapes. Lucas shivered. It was going to be a clammy night.

The side street on which the church stood was dark. No lights shone in the church or churchyard. As the three of them turned off on the darkened little lane, a man passed, glancing curiously at them. Lucas bit his lip. Della had warned him this area was all too public. At least the mist would mask any activity out past the main street.

I doubt that's a coincidence, Lucas thought, and shivered again.

They paused as soon as they got out of the streetlight. The mist seemed to muffle sound, and other than the occasional whoosh of a car passing along in the street behind them, they heard nothing.

"I don't see their cars," Lucas whispered.

"They probably parked in various spots in town so as not to be conspicuous and then walked here," Della whispered back.

Lucas nodded. That made sense. It also made it harder for the cult to escape. All the better.

They skirted the waist-high stone wall that bordered the churchyard until they came to the iron gate. It stood open. The distant streetlamps and ambient light from the surrounding town cast little light here. The church was a gloomy, featureless bulk. The gravestones were vague shapes dotting the slick grass.

They paused for a long moment, looking and listening, but detecting nothing. Della tugged on his sleeve.

"Come on," she whispered. "If we don't hurry up, they'll get done and get away."

Oh, they won't get away, Lucas thought,

suppressing a shudder. *Not from what they're about to release.*

He realized he did not feel guilty about leading Dr. Olding and her companions into mortal danger. It was self-defense or even war. If he didn't do this, a lot more people would be killed, people he cared about.

Yet still... he wished he felt a little guilt.

Whoever took your parents didn't feel any guilt, he told himself, *and neither do those bastards in the field.*

They entered the graveyard, moving between the headstones and crouching low to make themselves less visible. Their footsteps made little sound on the damp grass.

Halfway across, they stopped in their tracks as a faint voice called out somewhere ahead of them.

A voice replied, softer this time. They could not understand the words.

"That way," Della said, her voice barely audible. She pointed to a cluster of bushes and taller head-stones near the edge of the graveyard.

They crept to it, ears perked for more voices.

They heard none. Whoever was out in that field was keeping quiet now.

There was no wall surrounding the back part of the graveyard, only a narrow ditch with some water running at the bottom of it. They had a clear view of the field—or would have had one if it weren't for the mist.

If only they could see! Lucas could barely make out anything ten meters away. How the hell would they see what those killers were doing out in the field?

The answer was that they couldn't. They stood helplessly behind the bushes. All they could see was an expanse of grass disappearing into a milky haze.

"This is quite the weather spell," Richard said. "These people are advanced."

"What do we do?" Lucas asked.

"Wait," his friend replied.

Della pointed ahead and then a bit to the left. "The spots I pointed out to her are about fifty meters from here."

They all squinted. Nothing.

Then a soft sound came to them. It repeated, first from ahead and then a bit to the left. The sound continued from both points.

"Digging," Della whispered.

"I just had a horrible thought," Richard said.

"What if they actually do find an item of power at the points where Della indicated?"

"That would be just our luck," Lucas grumbled.

"Don't be ridiculous," Della said. "Can we call the police now?"

Lucas made a calming motion with his hand. "We haven't seen anything, and they still haven't started the ritual."

As if in response, a low chanting reverberated through the mist. The sound was subdued, as if the cultists knew that even with the cover of the fog, they still needed to keep quiet in the middle of this populated spot, but it also had force and came from many mouths. The whole group was assembled.

Good. It was time to finish this before more people got hurt.

Richard started unpacking spell materials from a satchel he had, whispering an incantation under his breath. Not for the first time in the past few days, Lucas wished he had learned more about applied magic. His aunt had forced theory and history down his throat, and Lucas had accepted that because it was interesting, and it was the only way to stop her badgering, but he had avoided the ritual side of the Craft as much as possible.

It felt too close to what had happened in his bedroom all those years ago.

They never found out just who had sent the dark spirit after his parents or why. All he and his aunt knew was that it was someone like the people out in the field.

Lucas couldn't stop the spirit that some twisted occultists had raised when he was a boy, but he could stop this.

And he would. He owed it to his parents not to let this kind of thing happen again.

He owed it to himself too.

The chanting continued, rising in force if not in volume. The summoning was reaching its culmination.

He could feel it. Glancing at Richard, he saw his friend could feel it too—a rising sense of power intermingled with a confused jumble of emotions. Richard sensed confusion, hope, a spark of awareness, and the sudden flare of anger.

"He's awake," Richard whispered. "They've brought him back."

Lucas didn't need to ask who. It was the Egyptian-Roman sorcerer, or his spiritual essence, brought back into consciousness by the ritual.

Someone out in the mist-shrouded field screamed.

"It's kicking off," Lucas said. "All right, Richard, Della, let's get this done. Della?"

When she didn't reply, Lucas turned to her, then looked all around.

Della was gone.

23

DELLA HAD no clear idea why she suddenly found herself in her car driving at dangerous speed through the mist back home to Oxford.

She only knew she needed to get back there.

Her thoughts were muddled, confused. She told herself it was a long-overdue panic attack, the continuation of the one she had the previous night, when she had come back from dinner with Whitaker and Dr. Olding and resolved not to see anyone for a couple of days.

But she hadn't gotten her rest. Instead she was yanked out of that by seeing Sebastian and then going to Lucas's house. A brief respite there, immediately followed by a stakeout in a misty cemetery trying to catch a murderous cult. Not exactly the silence and solitude she needed.

Let Lucas and Richard handle it. She wasn't needed. She wanted nothing to do with turf battles between made-up religions.

All she wanted to do was to get back home. Her apartment felt like a beacon in the night, a shelter that promised everything.

Della shook her head, trying to clear it, knowing she was being irrational but not having the will to seriously fight it. She blew a stop sign, overtook a truck that loomed suddenly out of the mist, and jerked back in her lane when headlights flared in front of her.

She should slow down, and yet she couldn't. Didn't want to. Her apartment awaited her.

The corner of her mind that always stayed aloof and rational, comfortably detached from the world around her, realized she was acting crazy. Was this a nervous breakdown? Had the increasing stress of the past few days finally reached a tipping point?

It didn't matter. Home was where she needed to go. Home had all the answers.

Somehow she made it without ending up in a fiery wreck. She got out of her car into a street shrouded in mist, the familiar houses changed into surreal shapes, the dark figure standing across the street unrecognizable and unnoticed as she fumbled for her keys and entered her building.

As she closed the front door she paused at the bottom of the stairs. The light was off. Only a feeble glow from the street came through the little fanlight above the door. The stairway was quiet, leading up into utter darkness.

Della let out a slow, easy breath. That darkness felt welcoming, a shroud of silent nothing that would shelter her from all the troubles and strife she had endured for the past few days.

She ascended the stairs without turning on the light. Not a sound came from any of her neighbors' apartments. The weak light from below barely reached her landing, her white door the vaguest rectangle before her. On instinct, she slipped her key in the lock on the first try, passed through the door, and locked it behind her.

The interior of her apartment was a bit brighter than the landing. The streetlight, diffused by the mist outside, shone in a uniform haze against her drawn white curtains. Their intricate lace designs were projected onto her walls and ceiling to look like blurred black cursive on a softly glowing bone-white background.

She dropped her keys on the side table, the metal making a disturbing clank that sounded loud and unwelcome in this silent space. Her gaze roved over the strange patterns the streetlight made through her curtains on the interior of her living room. Like writing.

Della smiled as she pulled off her sweater and tossed it on the sofa. Writing. All over her apartment. She had always found sanctuary in books, and now she was encased in one.

Books. That was what she needed. She needed to read. Drown herself in some obscure text and forget the troubles of the real world. It had always been her refuge, her escape when life got to be too much.

Lucas and Richard and the encounter at Alchester all but forgotten now, she kicked off her shoes and crossed the living room to the bookshelf where she had put the old volume Dr. Olding had lent her. She had read for a while before meeting Lucas and Richard at the pub. In fact, she had become so enthralled she almost missed that meeting. Della couldn't quite recall what she had read, only that it had soothed her, made her feel she had a place in this land. She was a foreigner but not a stranger. Her ancestors had come from England. She had returned home. And home was a place to be guarded.

As soon as she pulled the book off the shelf, she knew this was what she had come back for. In these musty pages would be the refuge she sought.

The rational part of her mind screamed in protest and was snuffed out.

Della sat on the sofa without turning on the light and opened the book at random. She brought the book close to her face and breathed in the smell of old paper.

Setting the book on her lap, she began to read the first sentence that her eye rested on. She did not question how she could read in such dim light and did not see the faint patterns on the walls and ceiling resolve into words.

"'Just as each place has its own *genius loci*, the spirit of that location, so does every land have a racial spirit. Would an Englishman ever feel truly at home in the islands of Japan? Or the steaming jungles of the Upper Volta? Would a Japanese or an African tribesman ever feel at home in the streets of London or the Yorkshire Dales? For each race its land. Any intrusion is against nature, and against spirit. The lone traveler or seasonal merchant does no harm, for he comes and goes with no intention of staying. It is the invader that kills the land. At this moment England is in a titanic struggle with its Gallic foe. If Napoleon takes England by force, he will impose French customs and French laws, and fill the villages and cities with Frenchmen. The spirit of the land will forever perish, as surely as the spirit of Rome perished under the weight of the Germanic onslaught.'"

Della nodded. This all made sense. Different countries were strong because of their differences, not their similarities. Change that, and the country is no longer that country.

The lines of text on her wall grew sharper. Della recognized this dimly, and it did not strike her as strange. Nor did the pool of black in the far corner of her room bother her. As it slowly expanded, she turned to another passage, even though the room was too dark for normal eyes to read. This, too, did not concern her. She was in the book's thrall, and all rationality had disappeared.

"'The magic of a land must be tapped by a practitioner of that land. Even if he is a foreigner to his own home, having traveled far and wide or having been born to native parents in another land, the true wizard will return to his true native land and take up the Craft. For the Craft has chosen that man or woman, and its call can be heard across great oceans.'"

As she read, the dark patch in the far corner grew and began to take shape.

Della turned a page.

"'Once the initiate has returned to the native land, those more skilled in the Craft will prepare the initiate through many methods either direct or cunning. Suitability is all that is required. The initiate need not have knowledge or belief or even the will to join the Craft, so long as the path has been prepared for them.'"

The shape in the far corner rose to full height and split in two.

"'Those experienced in the Craft will always recognize a suitable candidate, and will by many subtle and diverse means get the initiate into their thrall. Through careful preparation, the candidate's incorporation into the Craft is inevitable except for those of the strongest will.'"

Something made her look up. It was not the motion in the corner, which she had noted for some time, but more of a physical pressure, as if an invisible hand had taken her chin and gently but firmly raised her face away from her book and turned it in the corner's direction.

Two figures stood before her in the dim light, framed by the glowing walls and patterns of text.

One was an old crone. The other a burly man with a hammer in his hand.

Both extended a hand to her.

In the deep recesses of her mind, something trembled.

The rest of her remained calm. With a slow, deliberate motion, she set the book aside. After the briefest of hesitations, she stood.

The crone and the blacksmith motioned her forward.

Her mind felt like it was stretching, as if two strong hands pulled at it from opposite directions. One pulled her toward the two strange figures in her living room, and the other pulled her away, pulling her to safety.

The text on the walls began to glow.

Della took a step forward, her body obedient while the back of her mind started to scream.

The blacksmith held out a cup filled with some dark liquid.

Drink.

Drink and join us.

The crone's words came not as a sound but as a thought.

And as a command.

Della reached for the cup and took it. It felt strange in her hand, like bone. The edge was jagged.

She raised it close to her lips and felt the heat wafting off the liquid's surface. Della inhaled the bouquet as one would with a fine wine. The smell of the drink was rich and familiar.

Then, with startling clarity, she saw what she held.

A portion of a skull filled with blood.

The rational part of her mind snapped back into control.

Della screamed and flung the disgusting thing away. It parted the curtains and smashed through her window. The words shining on her wall danced and scrambled, losing their luminescence.

The crone and the blacksmith roared with anger.

The crone reached out with a gnarled hand, nails like claws, while the blacksmith raised his hammer.

Della screamed again.

She dove back onto her couch and vaulted over it just as the hammer came crashing down, thudding against the cushion with such force that one of the couch's legs cracked and the couch sank to one side.

The crone flew at her, actually flew over the couch, those claw-like nails reaching for her face.

Della dodged to the side, and the claws raked her shoulder.

She circled the sofa only to get cut off by the blacksmith. Again he raised his hammer. Della backpedaled then stopped. The crone was behind her.

Not just any crone. Mother Shipton.

Oh God, this is all real.

Suddenly, the door opened, and the light flicked on.

"Della, are you all right?"

Sebastian!

The crone and the blacksmith faded but did not disappear. Instead they shot straight for Sebastian, who cried out and raised his hands before his face.

"Stop!" Della commanded.

The figures paused, vague blurs that Della's eyes could not focus on.

"It's me you want."

It turned out that line only worked in the movies. The crone and the blacksmith rushed at Sebastian again. He screamed then lashed out.

Remarkably, the blacksmith staggered back. That made the crone pause once again, as if surprised.

"Get out of this house!" Della commanded.

The words echoed off the walls, gaining force.

She caught a brief glimpse of two pairs of startled eyes, and then the crone and the blacksmith rushed out the door, bowling Sebastian over.

Della leapt over him to the darkened landing. The figures had paused there, as if gaining strength now that they were away from the light.

"Get out!"

With a whoosh of air, they fled down the stairs and shot through the open front door, disappearing into the night.

Della stood on the landing, trembling and shocked. Those two had tried to kill her, and all she had to do was tell them to leave?

A groan behind her made her turn around.

Sebastian lay on the ground, blood welling out of a gash on his forehead.

24

LUCAS DIDN'T HAVE time to worry about Della. Dr. Olding and Whitaker had just raised a spirit they couldn't control, and if he and Richard didn't rein it in, there was no telling what it might do.

It was already doing enough damage to the cult members out in the field.

Screams tore through the fog, men and women crying out in terror and agony. A mingle of words came out of the night.

"I see it! It's coming!"

"Let's get out of here."

"Stay where you are! We need to draw a pentagram."

"Too late!"

"Marsha, is that you? Agh!"

Lucas pulled out the sorcerer's amulet. The real one. Richard rose beside him.

"Just like we practiced, my friend," Richard said.

They hopped over the narrow stream, climbed the few steps up the embankment, and strode into the field.

Lucas tried to keep it together as they walked into the mist, the screams guiding their way.

Lucas held up the amulet and began reciting a chant in Latin, one that his aunt and Richard had taught him. It was an old Roman spell, one intended to allay hostile spirits, a truce between the flesh and the spirit, an olive branch to the land of the dead.

As they walked forward, shapes began to appear in the mist. A few bodies, visible only as dark blots in the milky fog, lay twisted on the ground. They did not move.

A scream to their left told Lucas and Richard where to find what they sought. Lucas raised his voice in the hope that the spirit would come to him.

It did, far more quickly than he wanted it to.

A rush of air. The mist parted before a dark shadow that shot straight for them. Lucas and Richard dodged to either side as it passed between them. Lucas whipped around to see it coming at them again. He held the amulet aloft.

The shadow stopped right in front of him and resolved into the figure of a man.

He had the dark coppery skin, brown eyes, and wide face of an Egyptian. Lucas was startled at how much he looked like the modern Egyptians he had met. His head was shaved, and he wore a red tunic and matching robe bordered with hieroglyphs embroidered in gold thread. The sorcerer was short, barely five feet. This was no modern man.

Not a man at all, Lucas reminded himself. *Not for thousands of years.*

The sorcerer extended his hand for the amulet.

"If I give you this willingly, will you leave this plane of existence in peace?" Lucas asked. One did not have to speak a spirit's original language to be understood. Beyond death, every spirit could communicate with every other.

And with every mortal, if it so chose.

"Once I have finished with them," the sorcerer replied. The Egyptian's lips did not move. The words seemed to echo in Lucas's brain. "But I need help."

The mist began to clear now that most of those who had cast the spell to raise it were dead. Through the thinning haze, Lucas could see Whitaker and three others huddled in a hastily drawn pentagram about twenty meters away. They had made it with chalk on the grass, a candle at each corner.

All the other cultists were dead or had run off.

Lucas hesitated. The sorcerer's request was clear. He couldn't pass through the pentagram to kill the remaining cultists. A mortal would have to break it for him.

But that would be murder. Lucas had known there would be blood tonight. He had set it up so that the cult would raise a spirit and not be able to control it. He had justified it by telling himself that it would save more lives than it would take. The cult had to be stopped.

But the spirit had done the dirty work. Now he had to take a direct hand in it.

"I'll do it, Lucas," Richard said. "People like them have been killing people like me for a long, long time. And if they had gotten their way, they would have killed me and everyone like me in all of England."

His voice did not waver.

Richard strode over to the pentagram. Lucas and the spirit followed at a distance.

"No!" Whitaker cried out, raising his hands, that confident face shattered by fear. "Wait. I'll give you a million pounds. No, two million! I'll give you anything you want."

Richard stood at the edge of the pentagram.

"Anything I want?" Richard asked.

"Anything." Whitaker was in tears. His three remaining followers huddled on the ground around him, clinging to his legs like children.

"I want to live without fear of people like you."

Richard kicked a hole in the chalk outline.

The spirit rushed into the breach.

Lucas looked away from what happened next, but he could not stop himself from hearing.

Richard walked up to him, his features drawn. "We've got to get out of here. All this noise is going to bring the police for sure."

Lucas pointed to the far end of the field. "We'll cut out that way and loop around the field to the cars."

He made a quick survey of the dead bodies, checking each woman. Their wounds were horrific, but he had to check each of them.

He did not find who he was looking for.

Where was Dr. Olding?

25

ROUSING SEBASTIAN TOOK SOME TIME. The cut to his head, while it bled freely, didn't look too serious after Della had staunched it.

Remarkably, no one had come to the door to ask what was going on. Hadn't they made enough noise?

Then she remembered the most popular student band was giving a concert tonight. That was why she hadn't heard the usual noises when she came back earlier. Everyone was at the show. Hannah from the dig had invited her along, but she had made her excuses and forgotten all about it until now.

Della shuddered as she realized that she was completely alone in the apartment when she got attacked.

Attacked by what? And why had she been acting so strangely?

She was too confused to think about it right now. Sebastian needed help.

He was just coming to, looking around him.

"Are they gone?"

"Yes. You came at just the right time."

Sebastian struggled to his feet, and Della helped him to a chair.

"This place is a mess," he said.

Della surveyed the room—the broken couch, the smashed window, an overturned chair and lamp. The open door to the street let in a clammy breeze.

She didn't dare go down and close it. Instead she closed the door to her apartment and locked it.

"Who were they?" Sebastian asked.

Della paused. She wasn't sure how to answer that.

"Friends of Dr. Olding. Part of that cult. I must have left the door unlocked, and they came in."

"I didn't see them enter the building."

"You were outside?"

Sebastian nodded, then winced as the movement caused him pain.

"Yeah, I was... waiting for you."

"Waiting for me."

Sebastian managed a smile. "Shamefully close to stalking, I'll admit, but considering the circumstances I think I can be forgiven."

"How did you get in?"

"You gave me keys because you're always forgetting yours. Don't you remember?"

"Oh, right," Della said, putting a hand on his shoulder. Her characteristic forgetfulness had finally proven useful.

"What's going on? Is your professor's cult after you?" Sebastian asked.

"They're killers and completely crazy. They drugged me tonight and tried to get me to join them. My God, they tried to get me to drink blood from a skull!"

Sebastian studied her. "Drugged you? You look fine now. How did they try to drug you?"

Della turned to the book lying open on the broken couch. Lucas had warned her not to accept anything from them. She had thought a book would be safe. They must have put something on it to make her hallucinate. When she read the book for the first time earlier that evening, she must have gotten a small dose that compelled her to come back for more, like a junky returning for a hit. That would explain her crazy drive through the fog. Then she got a bigger dose just now.

Her shock was mingled with relief. Yes, it was some sort of hallucinogen. Lucas would have called it a spell, but it was a drug. A simple drug. Weren't these pagans always studying herbs and things like that? It had all been a trick. Two members of the cult dressed up like Mother Shipton and Wayland the Smith, trying to get her to abase herself in an initiation ritual.

And the skull with the blood? Had that been real?

Bile rose in her throat. Yes, that probably had. The scrapes along her shoulder from that woman's nails were real too.

"We need to call the police," Sebastian said.

"We will, but first ..."

She grabbed a washcloth from the kitchen, picked up the book, and holding her breath, carried it to the bathtub and threw it in. She yanked the battery out of the fire alarm, found a lighter, and set the book ablaze.

"What are you doing?"

Sebastian stood at the door, holding a cloth to his head.

"They gave me this book. Drugged it somehow."

"Aren't you destroying evidence?"

Della watched as the flames rose. The book crackled and hissed. She swore she could hear faint screams.

Just the drug, she told herself. *Just the last remnants of the drug.*

"I guess I am destroying evidence. But I want it gone. I'll feel... safer."

Sebastian opened a window and turned on the bathroom fan. The smoke blew outside as the flames consumed the last of the pages.

"Never took you for a book burner," Sebastian said, putting an arm around her.

"A lot has changed in the past few days. Let's call the police."

They heard footfalls on the stairs and a knock on the door.

"That must be Lucas and Richard!" she said, feeling immense relief. She rushed over, then paused, suddenly suspicious.

"Who is it?" she asked.

Silence.

"Who is it?" she repeated.

The door flew open as someone kicked it in.

Dr. Olding stood in the doorway. Her strange

pendant glittered. Her eyes blazed. But Della was more worried about the wickedly curved dagger gripped in her hand.

"You've ruined everything, you little bitch!"

Della tried to slam the door in her face, but Dr. Olding kicked it open again.

Della ducked to the side, the knife missing her by less than an inch.

A vase of roses flew through the air and smashed into Dr. Olding's face.

"Nice one, Sebastian!" Della shouted as she grabbed her professor's wrist.

Dr. Olding was only stunned for a moment. She wrenched her knife hand, trying to free herself, but Della clung on tight, so the professor used her free hand to punch Della in the face.

Della grunted, seeing sparks, but gripped the knife arm with both hands.

Sebastian rushed in, only to get a harsh backhand from Dr. Olding. He recovered quickly and grabbed at the knife as well.

Together, Della and Sebastian twisted her arm until she cried out in pain, and the knife dropped to the floor.

"Hold her down while I call the police!" Della shouted.

She let go and hurried to where her phone lay on the kitchen counter.

Before she made it halfway there, she heard Sebastian cry out.

She whirled around and saw her ex-boyfriend stumble back, coughing and blinking, trying to wave away a cloud of yellowish dust around his head.

Dr. Olding reached into her pocket and came out with another handful of the same dust.

But Della was ready. She grabbed a sweater that was draped over the back of the sofa and flapped it in front of her the instant Dr. Olding blew the powder at her.

The powder went straight back into Dr. Olding's face.

Her professor coughed and screwed her eyes shut, momentarily blinded. Della glanced at Sebastian, saw that he was still coughing and rubbing his eyes, and dove for the knife lying on the floor.

Dr. Olding, anticipating the move, lashed out blindly with her foot and kicked Della in the ribs.

She gasped, just barely managing to toss the knife across the room. Dr. Olding fumbled for her, grabbed Della by the hair, and yanked her head up.

Within a heartbeat, Dr. Olding was master of the situation again, pulling Della to her feet and getting her in a chokehold. With her free hand she fumbled in her pocket and pulled out a glass vial. Della's eyes widened as she saw it was filled with blood.

"I'm going to initiate you whether you want it or not."

Dr. Olding used her thumb to pop off the cap. Della tried to push away her arm, but the chokehold made her weak. The room was beginning to dim. Her lungs felt like they were on fire.

With a last effort, Della stomped on her professor's foot and struck at her face with both hands.

That loosened the chokehold and allowed Della to suck in a deep breath of air before Dr. Olding reasserted the pressure.

Della pushed backwards, moving farther than she anticipated as she forced them both onto the landing and bashed Dr. Olding into the far wall. The vial fell. Dr. Olding tried to grab it and stumbled over Della, screaming as she pitched forward and fell head over heels down the stairs.

Della pirouetted her arms, leaning crazily over the edge. With a sickening realization, she knew she had tipped over too far and was about to fall right after her professor.

Strong hands grabbed her and pulled her back from the brink.

Sebastian.

They both gasped when they looked down and saw Dr. Olding's twisted, broken form lying at the bottom of the stairs.

EPILOGUE

ONE WEEK LATER...

The questions were finally over. DCI Matthews had conducted his last interview with Lucas and the others. The few surviving cult members had been rounded up, and the cult's two murder victims—a Pakistani kebab van owner and a Bengali taxi driver —had been identified. Richard and Lucas had performed a ritual to put their spirits to rest.

And now they could rest too. The bandages were off, and the spell the cult had built was broken.

They still faced the charge of interfering with a crime scene, but they were told the judge would go easy on them in consideration of their help with the case. Richard and Lucas could each expect a stiff fine, nothing more.

DCI Matthews had also kept their names out of the papers, along with Della's. Lucas wondered how he had managed that. News of the cult and the multiple deaths had made worldwide headlines.

Richard and Lucas and Aunt Mary sat in the library, Richard with a stack of books by his side. He had been up to the house many times to borrow books. Uncle Philip was out in the field tending the sheep. He had had enough of occultism for a while and politely bowed out of the conversation after plying Richard with a double Scotch.

"Have you spoken with Della recently?" Richard asked Lucas.

"Almost every day. She's still trying to process what happened. She's managed to convince herself that the book was laced with drugs and that the spirits that attacked her were two cultists dressed as Old Mother Shipton and Wayland the Smith. That's what she told the police."

Richard chuckled. "That will keep DCI Matthews busy looking for two suspects who don't exist."

"Perhaps we should summon them to testify," Lucas said.

"Rather not. I don't think Wayland took to me very well."

"Della actually commanded them out of her apartment," Aunt Mary said. "That girl has considerable Talent."

"We all sensed it," Richard said. "How did she explain away that little anomaly?"

Lucas laughed. "That they got scared. She had already tossed the skull out the window, and Sebastian had shown up, so they ran off, fearing the police."

"It's amazing the mental contortions normals will make to shore up their narrow worldview," Aunt Mary said, then frowned. "The *genius loci* for the King Stone and Wayland's Smithy have been tainted. We need to do a series of rituals to cleanse them. Otherwise, the next time a practitioner uses those sites, it could have bad consequences."

"I'd be happy to help you with that in return for more of this wonderful Scotch," Richard said, raising his glass.

"You're incorrigible," Aunt Mary said with a motherly smile. "The three of us can get started tomorrow night with the King Stone. It isn't roped off as a crime scene."

"The two of you," Lucas corrected. "I have had quite enough of spell casting for the moment."

"Stop denying your true nature," Aunt Mary said.

"Leave him, Auntie," Richard said. "He did well and deserves a break. We can handle it ourselves."

"One thing I still don't understand," Lucas said. "Why did the spirits not dissipate when Sebastian came barging in to Della's flat? Those policemen showing up at Wayland's Smith certainly sent Wayland packing."

Richard shrugged. "The policemen were normals, and their presence disrupted Wayland's magic. Perhaps Sebastian has the Talent."

"Wouldn't you have sensed that?"

"I never approached him in those times he came to the Knight Errant. Nervous newbies aren't my style."

Lucas suddenly remembered an important detail. "Wait, Della said he hit Wayland, actually hit him. He must have the Talent. Perhaps you should talk to him the next time you see him. Check him out... um, I mean ..."

Richard laughed. "Lucas, are you asking me to seduce Della's ex-boyfriend?"

"No! Just see if he has the Talent."

Richard arched an eyebrow. "And if he does, I should initiate him?"

Lucas smiled. "I'm not saying anything that Della could hold against me later."

"Oooh, so you do like the little Yank, do you?"

"Feel free to stop at any time."

"Nonsense. Making fun of you is far too much fun. Auntie, get her up here right away. If he's going to laze about while we set the ley lines aright, at least he can do something to improve his love life."

"I don't fancy her," Lucas objected.

"It isn't up to you," Richard said. "You just sit there and look pretty."

"You'll do more than that," Aunt Mary told him. "You will invite her up to dinner."

"Oh, I don't want—"

"It's that or help with the rituals."

"Bloody hell," Lucas grumbled. "You two are unstoppable."

DELLA'S BUZZER RANG.

"Who is it?" she asked into the intercom.

Sebastian's voice came through the speaker. "It's me."

"Come on up," she said, her heart beating a bit faster.

Other than in a police interrogation room, she hadn't seen Sebastian since they had fought her professor a week before. They had not had time together to process what happened.

She had had plenty of time alone to work through it, though.

DCI Matthews had gotten her off the hook by proclaiming Dr. Olding's death an accident. She had fallen down the stairs, and the facts relating to that would not be brought up in court.

Della couldn't believe her luck. Of course the whole department was in an uproar. The loss of an important professor to a "freak accident" shocked everyone. Della had to endure countless conversations about what a wonderful person Dr. Olding had been and even attended a memorial service for her at Christchurch College chapel. Everyone took her expression of enduring horror to be one of grief. Fine by her.

The excavation, of course, was cancelled. Della and the others had suddenly found themselves without a summer job. That was going to put a crimp on her finances. She didn't care. She was finally getting her downtime. She could have the next several weeks to read and relax and work through what had happened.

A knock came at the door.

"Is that you, Sebastian?"

"Still me, yes."

She opened the door. Sebastian held a bouquet of roses in a vase. He no longer had a bandage on his forehead. The cut was healing well but would no doubt leave a scar.

Della felt like she had gotten a few scars herself.

Sebastian raised the vase a little. "To replace the one I bashed into your professor's face."

Della smiled. "Very thoughtful. Come on in."

Once he did so and Della had closed and locked the door, she put a hand on his arm. "I'm sorry I was so sharp with you."

"And I'm sorry that I was such a two-faced cad."

"It's just that relationships, even friendships, are hard for me. I felt betrayed, and I took it out on you more than I should have. I should have thought of your feelings too, so I'm sorry."

"And I'm sorry that I couldn't sort out my own feelings without mucking up yours. Instead of apologizing to each other all night, how about we make up for it somehow?"

Della hesitated. Was he making a pass?

No, you idiot, of course he isn't, Della told herself.

Della took the flowers from him. "I know, I'll cook while you go to Oddbins and get something nice, and I mean really nice." She emphasized this by poking a finger into his chest. "Then we'll eat, drink, and you can give me the best back rub you've ever done."

Sebastian put a hand on his heart. "I won't spend less than thirty pounds, and I'll limber up my fingers."

Della smiled as he went out the door, knowing she had forgiven him. While she wasn't quite sure how their friendship would develop after the failure of their relationship, Sebastian was too good of a guy to toss by the wayside. Plus he had been there for her when she needed him most.

Lucas had too, more than once. He had texted her earlier that day to invite her up to the farm for some of that fresh mutton he had boasted about. She had hesitated about saying yes. She had no doubt in her mind that he and his aunt would team up on her about learning more occultism. Even Uncle Philip would probably get in on the game.

But they were kind people, caring people, and she had resolved to stop keeping everyone at arm's length.

She'd just have to stand firm on the hocus-pocus.

She chuckled as she pulled out her cell phone.

"I'll come, but no spells."

Within a minute, the reply came—three happy faces followed by, "No spells, but my aunt wants to tell you the history of the house. I think you'll find it interesting. She'll probably try to lend you some books too. Don't worry, none will contain *genius loci*. Oh, I mean hallucinogens. How silly of me."

Della laughed. She'd never get him to see reason.

She reminded herself to ask Sebastian what kind of wine went well with mutton.

DCI MATTHEWS SAT in his office, staring at a mountain of paperwork. Police red tape was bad at the best of times, but with a multiple murder case, it rose to unbelievable proportions.

Not only that, but there were ties to at least two race-motivated murders, both done in a ritual manner, and the death of a leading university professor.

The university had come down hard on the police, insisting that the connection between Dr. Patricia Olding and the cult be kept from the press. They wanted the official line to be that she fell down the stairs while visiting a student. The university always got its way in Oxford.

Usually that rankled him, a bunch of toffs thinking they were above regular consequences. This time, though, he didn't mind, because if he hated anyone more than elite Oxford dons, it was reporters. Parasites, the whole lot.

He couldn't keep the press away from the ritual killings and the slaughterhouse at Alchester, but he could cover up Dr. Olding's connection to it. All the evidence pointed to Della Marshal acting in self-defense. That portion of the skull from one of the murder victims with Dr. Olding's fingerprints on it clinched the matter. Della had no choice but to kill her professor.

But that didn't make her innocent, not by a country mile.

She and Lucas Lancaster and Richard Camilo were up to something. They were in too many places at the wrong time. They hadn't been in that cult—in fact, they were instrumental in its downfall—but they knew things they weren't telling.

He'd keep an eye on those three. DCI Matthews had never had to deal with the occult community before, and he knew that any trouble among those people would no doubt bring Della and Lucas and

Richard running. He had a feeling he'd meet with them again, and this time he'd wring the truth from them if he had to grab them by their bloody necks.

Especially with those occult killings going on in London. If they didn't get involved in that in some way, he'd hand in his badge.

ABOUT THE AUTHOR

S.A. Beck lives in sunny California. When she's not surfing, knitting, or daydreaming in a hammock, she's writing novels.

www.sabeckbooks.com